F
MAZ

Mazer, Harry.

Who is Eddie
Leonard?

25302

$14.95

DATE			

WHO IS
EDDIE LEONARD?

WHO IS
EDDIE LEONARD?

A Novel by
HARRY MAZER

Delacorte Press

Published by
Delacorte Press
Bantam Doubleday Dell Publishing Group, Inc.
1540 Broadway
New York, New York 10036

Library of Congress Cataloging in Publication Data

Mazer, Harry.
    Who is Eddie Leonard? / by Harry Mazer.
      p. cm.
    Summary: A fourteen-year-old boy who was raised by
an abusive old woman and who has always had questions
about his parents sees a picture of a missing child and sets
out to discover if he is that child.
    ISBN 0-385-31136-2
    [1. Identity—Fiction.   2. Missing children—Fiction.]
I. Title.
PZ7.M47397Wk 1993
[Fic]—dc20   93-22114
                                                CIP
                                              AC

Book design by Barbara Berger

Manufactured in the United States of America

November 1993

10 9 8 7 6 5 4 3 2 1

BVG

For my editor Craig Virden,
for his unfailing and generous support

WHO IS
EDDIE LEONARD?

"The FBI lists 663,921 Americans as missing. Every six minutes someone new disappears. Sometimes they return in a few days or weeks or months. Five years is not unheard of."

The New York Times

PART I
EDDIE LEONARD

I am not me; I am someone else.
I am from another place.

ONE DAY WHEN I WAS ALMOST FIFTEEN I SAW MY FACE ON A POST office wall. This may sound like the beginning of some cheap little thriller, but it's the truth. It was on a poster for missing children. DO YOU KNOW THESE CHILDREN? One snapshot jumped out at me . . . JASON DIAZ: DISAPPEARED WHEN HE WAS THREE YEARS OLD. I took the poster down, folded it into my pocket and walked out with it. When I got home I pinned it up in front of a mirror and compared it to my face.

It wasn't a very good photo. It was smudgy and slightly out of focus. It showed a little boy with eyes round and nicely spaced, not too close, not too far apart. The left eye looked out at the world bravely. The right eye was a little sad. The lips were full. Solemn little frog face. I liked it. I liked that face. The more I looked at it, the more I knew it. It was a face I saw every day of my life. It was my face, Eddie Leonard's face, but attached to another name.

1

MY GRANDMOTHER LIED to me about everything. Big lies and little lies. The big lies were about my mother. The little lies were about everything else, like saying Siam listened to everything I said. "Ask him," she said.

I was three, maybe four years old. I got down on my hands and knees to talk to Siam, but he went under the bed. I pulled him out by the tail, and he scratched me. I cried.

"See," my grandmother said. "That's what you get for being a dumb, wacko kid. Turn the waterworks off! Stop that crying, you wetfly."

Or she'd suddenly say, "Listen! I hear something! What's that? Who's on the stairs? Sharon's coming! Don't run. Don't run. She's not coming if you run!"

I stood at the door, listening. I heard footsteps. I heard them come to the door and then go past.

I knew it was my fault my mother didn't come back.

If I was acting up, my grandmother would say, "Stop that

snotnose whining. You're as whacked-out as my daughter. She dumped you on me. She said she was going out for cigarettes. She was coming right back. You see her? You hear her? Where's your wacko mother, tell me?"

My grandmother said I didn't appreciate anything she'd done for me. I was an ungrateful greedy brat and she couldn't stand the sight of me. She said I made her dizzy the way I ran around. I made her head spin. "If you don't stop that jumping, I'll kill you. I can't think. Stop! Cut it out, you crazy thing. You dizzy, dopey, kid. You're killing me!"

I spun. I went faster and faster. I couldn't be touched. I couldn't hear her, couldn't see her. Round and round . . . I spun till the walls went one way and the floor the other, and I crashed into my grandmother.

"I'm dead!" she yelled. "I'm hemorrhaging. Are you satisfied, you little pig." I dove into the soft pillow of her belly, into her big soft belly. She didn't push me away. She held me hard against the cold metal button of her jeans.

If my grandmother was feeling good she'd tell stories about me and my mother. Funny stories. She'd say my mother found me in a garbage can in the park. Or on a park bench. Or in a hole in a tree. Every time she told the story it changed. Once she said my mother got me from a girl who delivered me to her in a baby carriage. The girl asked my mother to watch me while she went to the bathroom. "Sharon's such a dope she stood there and waited. The girl never came back and she was stuck with you. Sharon's always been that way. Put something in her hand, she'll hold it."

My mother's helpful, I thought. She likes to help people.

"Sharon's got her father's brains. He was gorgeous and dumb. He used to talk to himself and kiss at himself in the mirror. Sharon thought you were so cute, you were a doll, until she had to change your diaper. Then she came running home to Mama. She was screaming. It comes out like mustard, she said. What did she think it was going to be, sweet cream?"

"She came home with the baby carriage?" I said.

"What baby carriage? Aren't you listening to me? Sit up, pay attention or I won't tell you any more stories."

My grandmother had a friend named George. When he came to see her, she pushed her hair to one side and put on a lot of shawls and sprayed herself with perfume. "Don't embarrass me in front of my friend. Don't call me Grandma."

"Mama?" I said.

"No, you little idiot. I'm not your mother. Call me Lorraine."

My grandmother had George's picture on the TV next to Uncle Stew and my mother's picture. My uncle Stew lived in Florida. My grandmother said nobody knew where my mother lived. "She lives in cars. She lives in bus stations. She's on roller skates."

I held my mother's picture up to my face and looked at us both in the mirror. I had straight black hair and my eye brows were thick and dark as crayon. My mother's hair seemed to catch light. Light bounced off her hair everywhere. It caught in her shaggy bangs and on the tip of her nose. She was squinting and blinking as if the light was too much for her.

My grandmother said my mother couldn't stay in one place for long, and that's why she didn't come see me. She said Sharon was busy on her career. She said my mother was a dancer. No, an actress. No, she'd just won a beauty contest in Arizona. Or maybe it was California. Or New Mexico.

I spun. Dancers turned, they spun, they couldn't stop, they couldn't hold their legs still. They had to dance. I spun faster and faster.

"You idiot," my grandmother said. "What are you doing? Stop! You're giving me a headache. Stop, enough already. You're making my eyes fall out of my head. What did I do to deserve you?"

We lived in New Jersey, just outside Passaic, in a four-story apartment building, across the street from the Big M Market. Next to it was a dry cleaner and next to that was a liquor store and then another building where people lived. And another building, and another. In the morning, Siam and I would sit on my grandmother's bed and wait for her to wake up. Siam would step delicately over her. He'd swing his black tail in my face and I'd grab it. His ears would flatten and he'd hiss, and then Grandma would start kicking under the covers, trying to knock us off the bed.

"You see what you did, you wacko cat!" I said. "You woke her up."

She hated getting up in the morning. She watched TV late into the night. We watched the wrestling. She liked the big men banging into each other and pounding each other to the floor. She liked the body slams and the way they threw one another out of the ring. But in the morning it was hard for her to get up. "Grandma." I shook her. She'd pull me under the quilt. She'd hold me and wouldn't let me go. I'd lie there, buried under her heat and her smells, thinking of my mother. Did she ever hold me like this?

I had no memory of Sharon, but I did remember things. Things my grandmother said I couldn't remember. But I remembered. I remembered holding on to the hand of a big person. I remembered how still the darkness was and how noisy the day. I remembered whistles and bells. I remembered a room with red walls.

My grandmother worked in an office. Sometimes she was a bookkeeper. Sometimes she was the office manager. Once she brought me to work. It was a big room with a lot of women sitting at desks. They gave me cookies.

Sometimes she brought me places I didn't like. I remember not being fed, and kids being mean and being locked in a dark place.

Sometimes she would leave me with a family on the first floor. Doug and Lucy. They had a baby, Becca. I liked them, but my grandmother only left me there when she had to. She said Lucy had her nose in other people's business. Lucy liked to ask me questions. I didn't mind. She asked me why I called my grandmother Lorraine. She said, "Where's your mother?"

"Dancing," I said.

"She leaves you with your grandmother?"

"Uh huh."

"Do you like living with your grandmother?"

"Uh huh. I like George, too."

"Who's George?"

"My grandmother's friend."

"Does he come a lot? Does he stay with you?"

"Sometimes."

George had a big chin. "Hit me there," he'd say, sticking out his chin. He kneeled down. "Come on, punch me as hard as you can. On the chin. Give it to me right there."

I hit him as hard as I could, and he laughed. "You call that a punch. That's a kiss. Give it to me again. Harder."

For a while I thought George was my father. I was sorry

when he stopped coming to see my grandmother. I didn't like her new friend, Leon. He would lock my face between two fat fingers and squeeze until my lips popped out. "Lorraine, look at this clown," he'd say. "Doesn't he look like a goldfish?"

"Babies," my grandmother said, about her boyfriends. "Not one of them knows how to treat a woman." She looked around for her cigarettes. "They're just good for one thing. End of discussion. Shut up. You talk too much and you ask too many questions and you're a dizzy dope of a kid."

"I like George," I said.

"If you say George to me again, I'm going to tear your guts out and feed them to you."

When Leon stopped coming to see her she got into a bad mood. She didn't go to work and she didn't talk. "Don't bother me. Leave me alone. Nobody cares about me. I have a daughter without a brain and a son without a heart. If I died this minute, who'd care? Who'd come to my funeral?"

"I will," I said.

"Oh, you!"

When I tried to push her mouth up into a smile, she slapped me away. "Leave me alone, you pest." I tried to hug her, but she knocked me off. "Get out of here, go on, go outside. Scat, get run over."

WHEN I WAS SIX I started smoking secretly. Once she caught me smoking one of her cigarettes. "You're as good as dead," she said. "That's the size you're going to be for the rest of your life. You want to know why your mother doesn't come see you? She doesn't like smokers. Keep smoking, and you'll never see her."

"Why do you smoke?"

"Shut up," she said. "I do what I want."

She always left cigarettes burning on the edge of the counter. She left food out, sardines and beans in open cans with ragged edges for me to cut myself on. She left cupboards open for me to walk into. She left the window open for me to fall out of. We lived on the fourth floor. One day she saw me from the street, sitting on the windowsill, and she came screaming up saying the next time she was going to drop me out the window herself.

When I started school, kids would ask me about my father, and I asked my grandmother. "Your father? What father?" she said. Then she said, "He was a big man. B. B. Mellon. Big Boy Mellon. Big Bo, they called him." When I held my hand up over my head, she said, "Bigger than that. *Big*," she said. "He was a wrestler. Big John weighed two hundred seventy-three pounds. The way you eat, you're going to be in the cockroach class."

"John. His name is B. B."

"Stop bothering me!"

When we watched wrestling I kept saying, "Is that him?"

"Sure, that's him," she said. "That gorgeous hunk. That's him, Big Bo."

I stood close to the screen. I kept hoping he'd look at me. I wanted to press myself right in next to him. I told my best friend, Rick Brady, that my father was a wrestler named B. B. Mellon.

Rick pushed me. "Big Bo! I bet!" He hit me on the head.

"Big Bo!" I said. "He's got arms like a gorilla. Once he gets his hands on you, you're dead."

"What's his name, B. B. Watermelon? Does he look like a cantaloupe? I never saw him on TV."

"Shut up, wacko! My grandmother says Big Bo doesn't wrestle anymore. They're so scared of him they gave him a lot of money to retire."

Once, a big man came to our door. He was huge. He looked too big for the doorway. He wore a suit and he had a dark face and a smile like white lightning. I thought, *That's my father,* and I went back so fast I fell over. "Lorraine Leonard live here?" He had a leather case under his arm, and he was breathing hard. "I hate these walk-ups. Young man, you think I can have a glass of water?"

I brought him a soda. He was sitting on the couch, long shiny shoes big as rowboats on the floor. He sat there breathing hard. "You're a big boy," he said. He took a sip of soda. "What grade are you in?"

"Fourth." My heart began to go faster.

"What's your favorite subject?"

"Lunch," I said.

When he laughed he closed his eyes and his pink tongue came out. He wiped his mouth with a handkerchief.

He liked me. He thought I was funny. He laughed at my joke. It wasn't even my own joke. Rick Brady in school said it all the time. Lunch was his favorite subject and Carmella Ortiz was his favorite dish and his favorite activity was sleeping.

When my grandmother came home, the man talked to her about life insurance. "Life insurance, are you crazy?" she said. "What am I going to do with life insurance? Who's going to pay for it? You going to pay for it?"

"How about the boy?" he said. "Think of the future."

"That's all taken care of," she said. As soon as he was

gone, she yelled, "How many times have I told you, don't let anybody in the house when I'm not here." She smacked me for letting him in the house and smacked me again for giving him a soda.

2 "Here," my uncle Stewart said, giving me the puppy he was holding. "This is for you. Her name is Gloria."

I held the puppy and she peed on me. I threw her down. Siam hissed and ran to my grandmother's room and wouldn't come out.

My uncle had been living on the beach in Florida. He wore flip-flops, jeans, and a Hawaiian shirt. His dark hair was tied back in a little pigtail. He said he ate good all the time and went to the dog track every day. "It was a great life till my karma deserted me. I came back to see my favorite, dim-witted nephew."

I climbed up on the couch, got my arms around his neck and jumped on his back. I loved to hang on to him. He whirled me around till I went flying off.

Uncle Stew took my room and I slept on the couch. Sometimes I'd wake up at night and he and Grandma would be sitting on top of me, eating and watching TV. Uncle Stew liked to tickle my ear when I was sleeping or drop things in my mouth. I'd sit up and watch TV with them.

My uncle held Gloria up to my grandmother. "Kiss her, Mom."

"Get it away from me." The puppy was still peeing all over the apartment. My grandmother chased after her and beat her with a newspaper.

Uncle Stew kissed Gloria, then bit her ear till she cried.

"That hurts her," I said.

He grabbed me and bit my ear. He gave me a bear hug and rubbed his bristly cheek against mine. He liked to hold me down and tickle me under the arms or across the bottom of my bare feet. Just making the tickle motion would start me kicking. "Stop," my grandmother said and slapped me off the couch.

Uncle Stew took three showers a day and walked around in his jockey shorts and talked about getting purified and getting his life together again. If my grandmother didn't give him money, he took it out of her purse. When she said something about money disappearing, he pointed a finger at me.

"Did you go into my pocketbook?" she said.

"Why are you asking me?"

"Look at his face," Uncle Stew said. "Sneaky eyes. Do you believe that phony innocent look? How can you believe a face like that? Drop him in the garbage, Mom. Sharon dropped him on you. Drop him in the garbage before he cuts our throats with a kitchen knife."

"I didn't do it. Ask him."

Uncle Stew made a fist from behind my grandmother's back, meaning I would be killed and buried if I said another word.

My grandmother looked at me hard. "I can tell if you're lying," she said.

I picked up Gloria. "I'm not a liar."

"You better not lie to me." She slapped at me. I saw her

hand coming and jerked back. She caught me in the nose. The hurt came and the tears, and I cursed.

Uncle Stew sat there, laughing at me. "Come on, I'll buy you an ice cream. Don't be an itch. Come on, you're my pal." He got his arm around me and gave me a kiss.

When he was nice, I always forgot the mean things he did.

IN SCHOOL I told Rick a story my uncle told me about the money fish. "There's a fish in Florida, you catch it, and it spits out money. It walks on its tail. My uncle knows how to catch them. He says they only come up on the beach on moonlit nights. He knows how to grab them. They give him all the money he wants."

"Yeah! Yeah, really!" Rick said.

Another time I said how once some giant white gulls took my uncle for a ride. "They had a special sling he sat in and they held it up with their bills. They carried him to an island in the middle of the ocean. He lived there. The whole island was his."

"How did he get back?"

"A giant white shark swallowed him."

"How did he get out?"

"He lit a cigarette, like this." We were in the playground. I lit a cigarette and showed him how the shark started to cough, and coughed my uncle up on the shore.

I told the same story to Lucy from downstairs. She laughed. "He's a character, your uncle," she said. "How long is he staying this time? So he got you a little dog? How's your grandmother feel about that?"

"Good," I said, holding Gloria out for Becca to pet.

One day I asked my uncle about the room with the red walls. I knew it had something to do with my mother. "A red room?" my uncle said. "Maybe it was a bar you were in with her." My uncle had that certain look on his face: funny and mean. "Maybe it was a pet store. You know, the place she bought you. You were in a cage next to the puppies and parrots. She couldn't make up her mind between you and a parrot. The parrot talked better, but you were toilet trained."

"You and Grandma never tell me the truth about anything," I said.

"So don't ask me anything."

"Tell me about my mother."

"She doesn't like kids."

"She likes me," I said.

"Yeah, like your father likes you."

"My father does like me!"

"Sure. Everybody loves you. Come on, dinkhead, we're going out."

We went out to a place that made vegetarian pizza. My uncle never ate meat. We sat in the window and Uncle Stew made growly noises at the passing women. "Look at that action. Rrrrr!" Then he rapped on the window and motioned to a couple of girls. They came in. They both had curly hair. Uncle Stew said, "You girls want some broccoli pizza? Sit down."

"Broccoli pizza?" One of the girls made a face.

"It's the best. Ask my nephew. Is it good, nephew, or isn't it?"

"It tastes like my uncle's socks," I said.

"Your nephew's cute," one of the girls said. "Too bad you're not cute like him." She sat down next to me. "What's your name?" she said to me. "Do you have a girlfriend?"

I put my head on her shoulder.

"You want *me* to be your girlfriend?"

"Ohh!" The other girl made a sad face. "You don't want me?"

"You, too," I said.

Uncle Stew jumped up and down in his seat. "He wants both of you. That's my nephew! He learned everything he knows from me."

One day he left. He met someone who was driving to Tucson, Arizona, and decided to go with him. My grandmother didn't want him to leave. "I don't know why you're going. Who am I going to talk to now," she said.

Uncle Stew ran through the house, looking for money. "Cough it up, Mom. I'll pay you back, don't worry. I'll pay you back, you stingy old hag." He went through the drawers, her pocketbook, the closets, taking all the money he found. He looked under dishes, where she sometimes stashed money. He searched me, went through my pockets. Then he left with my grandmother's TV and Gloria under his arm.

"Where are you going? Leave Gloria!" I ran after him, but he didn't stop.

It was Saturday, and I kept waiting for Uncle Stew to come back. I looked for Gloria, but I never found her.

That was when I started thinking I didn't belong to this family. I was in my room. The window was open and I could hear the pigeons on the roof, and the light came and went as the wind lifted the shades.

I didn't belong to Uncle Stew. Or my grandmother. Or Big Bo. I didn't belong to any of them, and especially not to Sharon. My mother would have come to see me. She would have called or written. She would have remembered my birthday. Uncle Stew and Grandma were right about one thing. Sharon had bought me or found me someplace, or someone had handed me to her, and she had handed me to her mother.

I went up the stairs and out on the roof. Mr. Lozano's pigeons were in the wire cage, cooing. They were all looking at me, all those eyes like one eye. All of them cooing, saying, *Who, who, who, who are you?* . . .

3 In junior high, I never went home till I had to. In cold weather I stayed in school late. I'd scrounge hot bread or chocolate cookies in the Home Ec room. Then I'd go to the gym and shoot baskets. I'd try to see how far I could move from the basket and still get the ball to drop in.

The first basket in, I said, Good. The next I said, This is my lucky day. I didn't let myself think about missing. I had to believe I was going to make it. And if I didn't, I'd pretend I did.

If there were other kids in the gym we'd get up a game. I'd block, take the ball, elbow my opponent, cut around him. I liked to play hard, but if the gym teacher saw he'd blow the whistle on me. "Cut it out, Leonard! I saw that elbow."

"I'm just playing."

"Hey, Loud Mouth, when I say cut it out, I mean cut it out!" A couple times he threw me out of the gym.

One day after school I heard the chorus practicing in the auditorium. I sat in back and listened. I thought, *I could be in that chorus.* I liked to sing. I had a good voice. They were singing spirituals. The director, who was wearing a long red dress, went back and forth from the piano to the chorus, raising her arms. Left to right, from one side to the other, and everywhere she went the music swelled. When she leaped the voices leaped with her.

"Joshua fought the battle of Jericho . . . and the walls came tumbling down. . . ."

I liked the part about the walls tumbling down. I could see them falling. I knew about walls, all kinds of walls. Walls I wanted to see over and couldn't. Walls I wanted to get through and couldn't. Not real walls, not the brick walls on 28th Street. The walls in my life. Sharon. My grandmother. Walls that seemed to be inside me. I felt closed in, locked away from something I wanted that I couldn't even name. My real life, whatever that was.

". . . and the walls came tumbling down. . . . Yeah!" I was on my feet, singing and waving my arms around.

The director whirled around. "Who's that? This is a rehearsal. If you can't be quiet, get out."

THE WINTER I WAS fourteen, the doctor told my grandmother she had to stop smoking and lose weight. "Fat chance!" she said to me. "I don't inhale, and as for dieting, if I can't eat the food I want, I might as well die right now, this minute. Hand me a cigarette."

I handed her one and took one for myself.

"Who gave you permission?" she said.

I ignored her. It had been a long time since she could tell

me anything. I was bigger, and she wasn't what she had been. She wasn't well. She said it was the cold weather that made it hard for her. She'd call me to come downstairs and carry the bundles and on bad days even to push her up the stairs.

One day I found her lying on the floor. I said, "Get up." She couldn't get up. I called the ambulance and they took her to the hospital. They kept her overnight, then sent her home with a bunch of pills. After that, I did the shopping and fixed the food. I'd come home from school, and she'd have a list of things for me to do. She stopped smoking or at least she cut down. She never used to be afraid, but now she had to have a light on by her bed at night and all her pills nearby and a can of Coke to wash them down.

We played cards a lot. She hated to lose and she could still yell. One day, I'd just pulled the queen of hearts, and I said, "What do you hear from Sharon lately?" It just popped out. I didn't even know I was thinking about her.

She discarded a couple of cards. "Give me two."

I slid the cards toward her facedown. "Well, did you?"

"Did I what?"

"Did you hear from her?"

"I talked to her."

"You talked to her! How come I don't know about it?"

"You were sleeping. It was a collect call. She asked about you. She sends her love."

"Really, her love?" I threw down a couple of cards. "She's a sweetheart. How come she talks to you and never talks to me?"

"Will you cut the gab and play your cards."

The cards went back and forth.

After a while, I said, "I suppose she's still dancing."

"I don't know what she does."

"Your own daughter and you don't know anything about her?"

"What are you, being sarcastic? What's this stupid conversation supposed to prove?" She tossed her cards in my face. She was losing anyway. "Get out of here! I don't like this. Where did you get that mouth?"

I picked up the cards. "From you, Grandma. Come on, tell me something real, not that stuff you used to hand me. Who's my father?"

"How do I know? You're Sharon's brat. I don't know who she picked for your father. I sacrificed my life for you, and you've got the nerve to harass me when I'm a sick old woman."

"I'd just like to see my mother."

"I can't make her appear out of nowhere, Eddie. If she doesn't show up, she doesn't show up. What do you care about that turkey, anyway? I brought you up. Now I'm not good enough for you?" She shuffled the cards. "You want to play or not?"

I looked at her gray face. Her hair was uncombed, her skin was loose and without color. "Deal, Grandma," I said. "I'm feeling generous. I'm going to let you win tonight."

The next morning, before I went to school, she told me she'd had pains all night long, but she wouldn't let me call the doctor. "I'm not going to the hospital and let them torture me. You can take care of me." It was the last day of school before winter break. When I came home that afternoon, she was groaning and grabbing at her chest.

"I'm going to call the ambulance," I said.

"Forget the ambulance. Will you sit still for a minute and

talk to me. Hold my hand. Not like that! That's mush. Really hold it! My God . . . what a stupid business." She was muttering to herself. "You're going to die, Lorraine. Stupid way to die."

She fell asleep and when she woke up she wanted a mirror and her hairbrush. She asked me if I saw gray in her hair.

"No."

"Oh, what do you know." She ran the brush through her hair. Then she wanted her makeup, and she put on so much gunk she looked like a clown.

Later that night I woke up and heard her groaning. I went to her. She had her hand on her chest. "Sit. Don't go away." I sat in a chair next to her bed. I tried to stay awake but I kept dozing off.

"Eddie, help me. Oh, God, help me. The pain's so bad."

I woke up and called the ambulance.

They strapped her on a stretcher and carried her downstairs. She lay with her eyes shut, not making a sound.

At the hospital they rushed her away.

I found the men's room and washed my hands and face.

A man in a plaid jacket came in and stood behind me, carefully combing his hair down over his eyes. "You okay, kid? You look kind of green."

"My grandmother's sick."

He nodded, as if he knew all about it. "She's going to be okay."

The nurse at the desk told me to go home. "Your grandmother will be here for a while," she said. "Go home and get a good night's sleep. Call us in the morning."

Outside it was cold and snow was falling. I thought about taking a cab, but I didn't have enough money, so I walked home instead.

IN THE MORNING I called Rick. His mother answered the phone and said he'd gone to visit his father in Chicago. I called another guy I knew, but no one was home. So I talked to Siam. "You notice anything different?" Her ears twitched. She was old now and she didn't jump around the way she used to. "Don't worry, she's just going to be in the hospital for a couple of days."

I went to the hospital to see my grandmother, but they only let me stay for a few minutes. "Grandma." I stood by the bed. There was a tube taped to her nose and another threaded into the back of her hand.

She opened her eyes.

"Grandma?" I didn't know what to say to her. I thought she was going to die.

She mumbled something. She didn't have her teeth in, and I couldn't understand what she was saying. I finally figured out she was talking about Uncle Stew. She wanted me to call him. She told me where she kept his number. She held my hand and told me to bend down, then whispered into my ear where the bank card was and her secret code. "You get Stew. You tell him he's got to come back. I'm going to need help."

I tried Uncle Stew's number. It rang a few times and then I got a recorded announcement. The number had been disconnected.

WHEN LUCY FROM downstairs found out that my grandmother was in the hospital, she invited me to eat with them a few times. I liked being with her and Doug. Becca was eight now, and they had a baby, Shannon. If you said her name she shrieked and kicked her feet. I baby-sat for Doug and Lucy sometimes. Not for money. They were my friends. I watched the way they were with their kids, sort of matter of fact, not fussing over them, but not screaming, either. They never screamed. It was the way I was going to be, I thought, if I ever had kids. And I'd want somebody like Lucy for my wife.

I was asleep when the phone rang. I squinted at the clock. It was 1:30 in the morning. "This is Dr. Maloff from the hospital. Can you get right over here?"

At the hospital, Doctor Maloff led me down the corridor He was wearing wrinkled greens and yawning. He told me that my grandmother was dead. "We went in to check her, and she was gone." He put his hand on my shoulder. "I'm sorry."

I stood outside the room and looked in. I saw her hand move, and I thought the doctor had played a trick on me, the way Uncle Stew used to, making believe he was hurt, then grabbing me when I started to cry. I went in.

"Grandma. I'm here." I thought in a moment she'd sit up and say, *Where were you when I needed you, you wacko kid?*

"Grandma, I came as soon as I could. I took a cab."

I know her tricks, the way she would lie in her bed, humped up, just her mop of gray hair showing on the pillow, like she was dead asleep. Then she'd rear up and kick me and Siam off the bed.

I HEARD A LITTLE pumping sound, like a faucet dripping. I put my hand on my grandmother's bare shoulder. Her skin was cool. I pulled the sheet up over her. Her feet stuck out. She had a thick callus on the ball of one foot. All her toes were squeezed together. I jiggled her foot, made it hop up and down, but when I stopped, her foot stopped.

When I left the hospital, snow was falling. It was all around me, ahead of me and behind me and coming down on me. I went home that way, closed in by the falling snow.

4 THE DOOR TO MY grandmother's bedroom was partly open. I walked by it ten times. Then I went in my room and opened the window and looked down on the street. On both sides, cars were parked and double parked. It was early. I climbed out on the fire escape and sat there.

I watched people going to work and kids going to school. It was the first day back. After a while, I went inside and got ready for school, but when I went out, I changed my mind and went to the hospital instead.

A guard stood by the elevators. I found the stairs and went up to the sixth floor. Near my grandmother's room, the corridor was crowded with wheeled gurneys. But my grandmother's bed was empty.

I went down the stairs, and out on the street. There was something inside me, something tight, that wanted to break out. Something hard that wouldn't let go. It wasn't my grandmother. It wasn't that. I didn't feel a lot, no tears, there was no catch in my throat. No, what I felt, that hard thing, was fear. *You're alone,* it said. *You said you were alone. Now you really are, and you can't stand it.*

5 I DIDN'T LIKE living alone. I had nobody to answer to. Whatever I felt like doing I did. I ordered up pizza at midnight then stayed up watching the late movie. It sounds great, but it wasn't. In the afternoon, after school I played arcade games. Then I went home to feed Siam. Then I slept. When I woke I went out again. I saw every new movie that came to town. Some weekends I'd see one movie after another. I came out of the mall sometimes and I didn't know who or where I was. I had to run to shake off the feeling. I ducked and dodged through the streets. I felt invisible, like a gray ghost.

I knew I was looking for something, but I didn't know what it was.

The only person I talked to about my grandmother was my friend Rick, but he wasn't very interested. He liked to talk about TV shows. He definitely didn't want to hear about the funeral. When I told him about it, I made it better than it was. I said people came and there was a service, but there was really nothing. The funeral people took care of everything. They got my grandmother's body from the hospital and put it in a box and put it in the ground and took the insurance money to pay for it. About a week later, someone called from Social Services. I said my uncle would call her back. "He's working," I said. I had my grandmother's money card and the code number she'd given me way back when I'd started doing the shopping.

I went to school almost every day, but it was hard for me to concentrate. My mind would drift off. I'd think my mother was home waiting for me. Maybe there was a note under the door. *I was here, but you were gone.* Signed *S* for Sharon. The single letter, big and sprawled across the paper.

But when I got home there was only Siam, waiting at the door. He slept with me and rubbed up against me. He'd always been my grandmother's cat. He still went meowing through the rooms calling her.

I OFFERED LUCY and Doug my grandmother's apartment. I was serious. I thought they'd ask me to live with them. It would be good for them and good for me. I could sleep in the living room or anywhere. I'd help them with the kids. I wouldn't be in the way. If they wanted me to take a walk so they could have a fight or something, I'd vanish.

They came up and looked around. I could tell they liked the apartment. There was a lot more room up here and more light. Their place was dark and cramped. The kids had the bedroom. Lucy and Doug slept in the living room on a pull-out couch.

"This place could be a palace," I said.

"What would you do?" Lucy asked. "Where are you going to go?"

"I thought I'd stay here with you. I wouldn't be in the way

or anything. I'll paint the apartment for you. You know Rubino will never do it."

Lucy and Doug exchanged a look.

"I know you have to talk about it," I said. "Take your time."

"Isn't someone supposed to come and help you?" Doug said.

"Yeah, my uncle Stew." I'd never told them that when I called the number in my grandmother's book, it was disconnected. "But he won't hang around."

"Maybe we better wait till he comes," Lucy said. "You know, Eddie, it's a lot of stairs to go up and down every day with kids and groceries and bikes, the whole bit."

Then she said I could eat with them any time I wanted.

One evening I went down to Lucy's. I was just going down to tell them something, and I must have left my door open. When I got back upstairs, Siam was gone. I thought he was out in the hall. "Siam?"

I went down the stairs calling him. I went outside but I couldn't find him. He didn't come back that night; or the next day. I kept expecting him to come back. I thought when he got hungry, he would come back. Lucy said I should put up a notice in the Laundromat.

After I did that, I walked over to the post office. Just inside the door where all the notices were, I saw a missing children's poster with photos of six missing children. One of them was of a three year old whose name was Jason Diaz. It was just a smudgy face on a poster. JASON DIAZ. DO YOU KNOW THIS CHILD?

Something in me said, Yes.

I took the poster down and folded it into my pocket. Then I put up a notice about Siam and walked out.

6

I LEFT THE POSTER on the kitchen table, still folded. Every day I walked by the table and thought about unfolding it. I knew I was going to do it, but I kept putting it off. I was waiting for a sign. I thought when Siam came home, I'd open it.

One day I went into the library on Market Street. I had put up a notice on the bulletin board about Siam and I went to see if it was still there. On the bottom someone had written, "Sorry! I love cats, too."

I asked the librarian if there were any more bulletin boards and she said there was one in the reference room on the third floor. I went up there. I was fooling around with one of the computers, when a librarian came by and asked me if I needed any help.

I said, "How do you find out about somebody?"

"Somebody famous?" he said.

"No. Some kid who's missing."

"If it was in the newspapers, we can check that."

He showed me how to search the newspapers. I tried the name first, Jason Diaz, but there was nothing.

"Search some other headings," he said. "Try looking under Missing Children or Kidnapping."

I spent a couple hours reading stories about missing kids. There were a lot of them, but nothing about Jason Diaz. Then I hit the jackpot, an article written a couple of years ago about what had happened to the families of kids who had disappeared. I was scanning it on the screen when I saw the name Diaz.

Jason Diaz had disappeared a few days before his third birthday and ten years later he still hadn't been found. He came from a town near the Canadian border. His mother was a music teacher and his father was a dentist. The girl who had been baby-sitting Jason had gone into a store and left him outside in his stroller. When she came out, he was gone. That was twelve years ago. Jason would be fifteen now. My age exactly. Before I left, I made a Xerox copy of the article.

When I got home that afternoon, I unfolded the poster and taped it to the edge of the mirror. For a long time I just stood there looking at my face and comparing it to the face in the poster.

It wasn't a very good photo, smudgy, slightly out of focus. It showed a little boy with round eyes spaced nicely, not too close, just right. The left eye looked out at the world bravely. The right eye was a little sad. The lips were full, too full. It was little more than a baby's face. A solemn little frog face. It was a face that was familiar. I knew that face. The more I looked, the more certain I became. I knew that face as well as I knew my own. It was a baby face, a baby version of a face I saw every day of my life. It was my face, Eddie Leonard's face.

I held the poster to my face. I held it so close that the picture seemed to tremble and fade away.

I belong to that face. I belong to a family. I belong somewhere else. Not here. Not to my grandmother who's gone, not to Sharon who never was, not to Uncle Stew, who never came. . . .

Somewhere a family was waiting for me—a mother and a father, maybe a brother or brothers. . . . I wanted to know them. I wanted to know what that face knew. I wanted to think what it thought.

I didn't know who I was anymore or where I belonged or what I would do. I only knew I was someone else. Not Eddie Leonard.

PART II
JASON DIAZ

Do you know who your parents are?

7

THE HOUSE AT Number 10 Walcott Street was white with green shutters and a porch that ran the width of the house. It stood at the edge of downtown, so Miller could always walk or bike everywhere and never had to beg her parents for rides, the way her friends did. Her parents were divorced, but her father's office was still in the house, so she saw him every day. That was the important thing. In some ways it was almost like he'd never moved out.

The sign on the front lawn said BRUCE DIAZ, D.D.S., HOURS 9–5 M–F. One day, she thought, her brother Jason would come down Walcott Street, as she was coming down the street now, and he'd stop and read the sign and know he was home. She tried to think of her brother as real but she never could. *Her perfect brother.* She couldn't imagine him with the faults she had. He was like his picture —always three years old, always smiling and cute and adorable. Even his faults were perfect. Her mother loved to tell how she could never keep shoes and socks on his feet. She'd put them on, and he'd pull them off. A perfect fault.

Miller entered the house. How could she resent a brother she didn't even know? Jason was beyond doing anything wrong. He'd gone away and was as unreachable as a star in the sky. Nothing could touch him. You could only look at him and wonder. *Look at that beautiful star. Look at Jason.* And you had to say it in a special voice, because Jason was special like nobody else.

She burst into her father's office. "Dad?"

"You know he leaves early on Thursdays," Roz, her father's receptionist, said. "He said for you to call him when you come home. Your Mom left at three o'clock."

Yes, Miller knew. Her mother was in Cincinnati for a music conference and master class for brass instruments.

Miller paused on the stairs. She hated coming home to an empty house. She hated not seeing her father. Of course, her mom would be just as happy never to see him. Miller remembered from before the divorce, waking in the night and hearing her parents arguing.

They didn't fight that way now, but when they were together, in the front hall where they did most of their talking, her mother would sit on the stairs with the ashtray on her knee, and her father would do his stretches—working on his back, he called it—only pausing to push the smoke away from Miller's face.

Sometimes, after one of these talks, Miller's mother would be so exasperated she'd say, "We're moving, Miller. I don't have to stay in this house another minute. You and I can live anywhere." But it was just talk. Miller knew her mother would never move. This was the house where Jason was born. This was the house he disappeared from. And this was where he would return some day.

"Miller," Roz called. "You're dragging your jacket. You don't want to make your jacket dirty, Miller."

Miller tossed her jacket over her head. "Roz, I want it dirty." She couldn't resist. "I want it slimy, disgusting, and filthy." She looked back. Roz was giving her a weary, indulgent look.

Upstairs, Graham waited at the door. He nosed into her, rapping her with his big bushy head. "Wait a minute, Graham. I know you want to go out." She found her mother's note in the kitchen on the refrigerator.

She got a bag of corn chips and sat down on a stool to read the note. The phone rang. It was Mary Anne. "How are you, honey? Did you just get home?" Her stepmother was always nice. But Miller never thought that without adding, "Too nice."

How could anybody be too nice? But that was Mary Anne. No, that was Miller—always criticizing, always finding fault.

"How was school today, honey? Are you coming over later?"

"I'm not sure. Maybe."

"We'll all be so disappointed if you don't come over. Why don't you come? I'm sure your father would come get you. Wait a minute, Mill, your father's just coming in from his run."

"Hi, honey," her father said coming on the phone. He took a couple of deep breaths. "Sorry I missed you. You were late."

"I was having a horrible fight with Francesca."

"We're going out to eat later. I'll come by and pick you up."

"Where are you going?" But that was just a stall. They

always ate at the country club Thursday night. It was the only place they ever ate. She thought about sitting with Mary Anne all night and being perky and nice back to her, and said, "Dad, I don't feel like going out."

"You're going to stay home alone? I don't know why your mother has to go away so much."

"Dad. You know, Mom has a gig."

"Call your friend and have her come over. I don't like you being alone in the house."

"You're not paying attention, Dad. I just told you Francesca and I had a big fight."

"I heard you. It was a horrible fight, right? Big fight, big deal. Make it up, honey. If you change your mind in the next half hour, call me. I'll see you tomorrow in the office, and don't forget Sunday. We've got a date for Sunday brunch."

As soon as she hung up Miller realized she had just cut off her nose to spite her face. Just because she didn't want to see Mary Anne, she'd ended up not seeing her father, either. She liked to see him every day. Her father was special. She loved being with him and talking to him, even though half the time his mind was somewhere else. She was always saying, "Dad, you're drifting off. Dad, are you listening to me? Hello, Dad!"

And he'd say, "Of course I'm listening," and he'd play back exactly what she'd been saying, even though she knew he hadn't heard a word. But that was only sometimes. Mostly, they had really good talks, because her father didn't hold anything back. He didn't treat her like a kid.

Just the other day they were talking about Jason again, and he got very emotional. "Your mother still thinks I didn't do enough to find him. I want him back as much as she does.

I went to California. I went to Mexico. I went to Canada. I can't spend my life looking for him. I would if I could, but I still have to work. You know what the police told us, honey. He's going to show up. Someday, he's going to show up. As long as they don't find—you know."

And she'd said, "I know, a body."

That's when he broke up. "Honey, it's tough," he said, "it's tough on you, it's tough on all of us."

She leaned against him. "It's okay, Dad." Those were the moments when she loved her father almost more than she could bear.

Miller got something to drink, then called Francesca. "Hello, this is your perfect friend, doing what perfect friends do, forgiving you."

"You're forgiving me? I forgive you!"

"What are you doing?"

"Nothing."

"Me, either. My mother's gone."

"Mine, too," Francesca said. "Gotta go now. I'm making supper. Love you. I'll see you in school tomorrow."

What had started their friendship was that they were both single daughters of single mothers. That was sort of stretching things, of course. Miller's father was right there, but still it got Miller and Francesca together. The other thing they had in common was that Francesca didn't broadcast that her mother had never married—it was like Miller's not talking about her brother. When people found out about Jason, they'd sometimes say really mean things, as if it was her parents' fault that Jason was gone.

Miller had never even told Francesca about Jason, until a year after they became friends. When she did, she told Francesca the story first, and she could tell that Francesca hardly believed her. She took Francesca to Jason's room. It was next to hers, and the door was always kept closed. "This is my brother's room," she said.

"Open the door! I want to see."

Miller held Francesca back. "I never open this door without thinking that my brother's in here." She let the door swing silently open. The room wasn't a shrine or anything like that. The baby furniture was gone. There was a bed and a bureau. The only thing special were the flowers her mother kept in a vase next to Jason's framed picture.

She and Francesca sat on the floor and looked at all the pictures of Jason her mother kept in an album. "What would you do if he walked into the house right now?" Francesca said. "Would you recognize him?"

"Yes, I would."

But would she? Jason was fifteen now. Miller looked at the older boys in school sometimes and wondered which one was like Jason. She couldn't imagine her brother like any of them. None of them was good looking enough or smart enough or nice enough to be her brother.

Later, when she took Graham out for his walk, instead of going down the street he dashed for the carriage house. It was just an old fancy garage with a loft upstairs where they kept a lot of junk. Graham ran inside and started barking up the stairs.

"Graham, what is the matter with you?" Miller said. "Is there a raccoon up there again? Come on, let's go, Dad'll take care of it." But he didn't stop barking. She had to grab him and pull him away.

When they came back, she fed Graham, then made herself a cheese sandwich. She stood by the window in the kitchen, eating and looking out into the yard. The carriage house doors were shut. She didn't remember shutting them when she dragged Graham out. Well, she must have. But still, she felt uneasy and went around the house and checked to see if all the doors and windows were locked.

8

I WRAPPED UP in a rug I'd found under the eaves and looked out the window. Through the bare branches of the trees I saw the high flat back of the house. *I'm home.* I kept perfectly still, concentrating. *Yes, you've seen this view before. You've looked through this window. You've stood here and looked down at the driveway and up at the house.*

It had taken me three days to get here. I caught rides in cars and with truck drivers. My last ride was with a Canadian truck driver in cowboy hat and boots, bound for Montreal with a trailer load of steel wire. Early this morning, he'd dropped me at a truck stop at the edge of town. The mountains were near and it was cold.

I walked into town, down wide windy streets. There were trees and flowers, and everything clean. The houses were painted white—no rust, no stains, no broken porches, no blocks of boarded-up factories. I saw cats with collars. Dogs wagged their tails. Everything was like a dream, like a picture in a magazine. *You're here,* I kept saying to myself. *You're here, you've come home.*

I wanted to make this place mine. I was still dazed. I waited for the town to descend on me and wrap around me and become part of me. I wanted to be able to walk every street with my eyes closed. I wanted to know every store, recognize everyone I saw. I wanted to be able to greet them and have them greet me. *Hi, Jason, how're you doing?*

I found my family's name in a phone book at a convenience store. There were three listings, two for Bruce Diaz—one at 10 Walcott Street and the other in a place called Rockhill. The other Diaz was Connie Miller Diaz at the same Walcott Street address.

I found Walcott Street. I found the house, but I didn't stop. I was rehearsing what I'd say. *Hi, Mom and Dad. I'm home.* But a giant hand seemed to be pushing me away. I went around the corner and came back again. I was talking to myself. *I believe. I believe. I'm Jason. I believe. I believe I'm home.* I stood outside, waiting for the miracle. Waiting for them to come out and see me and bring me in. But nobody came.

Later, when it got dark I stood in the trees behind the house. There were a few lights on. I willed myself to remember things. *Remember playing in the driveway, remember lying on the grass.* The earthy, sweet, rotten smell of apples rose around me.

I found a door open in the garage and went up to the loft. I was poking around when I heard a dog barking down below. Then a girl's voice calling "Graham!" I watched them going down the driveway.

All night each time I turned, I smelled mice and remembered the mice who lived in my grandmother's stove. And how the smell came up whenever she lit the oven.

SUNLIGHT WAS COMING IN when I woke. Birds chattered. I felt around for Siam, then I remembered where I was. I thought, Today is the day you're going in there . . . *Let me introduce myself. You may not know it, but I'm your long lost son, Jason Diaz.*

Maybe my father would open the door, with my mother behind him saying, "Who's that?" And both of them with their arms out, wanting to embrace the son who had been lost.

A car drove into the garage. A car door slammed. Out the window, I saw a man walking toward the house. He stopped to pick up a scrap of paper. I wanted to shout down to him. *Who are you? Are you my father? It's me, Jason.* He'd think I was a bum. He'd gag when he saw me. *My son? Pheew, what a stink!*

I got my knapsack and slipped out the side door and went through the wooded lot to the street in back. There was a convenience store nearby, on the main street. In the men's room I stripped down and washed myself. I used paper towels to scrub my neck and under my arms. I soaped my hair and rinsed it. I changed into clean jeans and a shirt and my good sweater.

I bought a couple of candy bars and a carton of milk. As I gave the money to the woman behind the counter I thought she was looking at me as if she knew me. I wanted to say something to her: *Do you remember me? Jason Diaz?*

I stood outside and ate a candy bar. Cars came and went. People greeted each other. It was a friendly place. Several people looked at me and I nodded, and they nodded back. My stomach kept clenching, but it wasn't for food. I wanted these people to know my name, know me. *Oh you're Dr. Diaz's son. I remember you when you were a little boy.*

I went back to 10 Walcott Street. I went up the front steps, counting. One . . . Two . . . Three . . . There were two glass doors. Then, a little hallway, and two more doors. Two bells. The top one for Dr. Bruce Diaz. The other for Connie Miller Diaz.

I hesitated. A man and a young girl came up behind me, rang the doctor's bell and were buzzed in. I followed them. I stepped into a waiting room. I was only dimly aware of the man and the girl, the chairs ringing the room. With each step forward, I felt something pulling me back.

"Hello, can I help you?" There was a woman behind a reception desk and behind her a wall of color-tagged files. "Are you here to see the doctor?"

I nodded.

"What's your name? Do you have an appointment?"

I shook my head.

"Doctor is all booked this morning. Friday's a very busy day for him." She flipped pages in a book. "I can make an appointment for you next week."

"I just wanted to speak to Dr. Diaz."

"Are you in pain?"

"It's . . . personal," I said.

"Who should I say?"

"Who? Just tell him I'm here—"

"I have to have a name."

"Eddie, I mean Jason."

"One minute." She went down the hallway. I heard her say, "Eddie Jason wants to see you." Then a man's voice. "I don't know anyone by that name."

I looked down the corridor. I saw the man from the car. He was wearing a short white jacket. He had a little curl of hair in back neatly tied back with a string. It was my father. He looked up and saw me, nodded, then disappeared into another room.

"You'll have to make an appointment," the nurse said coming back. "Doctor's all booked today." She looked down at her book.

I stood there for a moment, then left.

On the street, my feet flew over the ground. I was hot, like I was bulked up with a lot of extra sweaters. My lips were throbbing. I walked, I kept walking. I passed a library, a round stone building, and went in.

A boy behind the counter looked up. "Yes?"

"Can I use the library?"

"Do you have a card?" He gave me a form to fill out. I wrote Jason E. Diaz. E for Eddie. Then I erased it. There was no Eddie anymore. Only Jason Diaz. I put down my father's address.

"Have you got any ID?"

I patted myself. "I must have left it home."

"Bring it next time."

I signed the back of the card. Jason Diaz.

When I left I had the card in my hand and as I walked, I looked at it. Looked at my name. Looked at my signature. Jason Diaz. So it wasn't so bad. Things weren't ruined. I had gone to the house, I had stepped into my father's office. I could have talked to him. I didn't because I didn't want to do it in front of other people.

I stood outside the convenience store, to use the phone. I turned a coin between my fingers. *Let there be no doubt.* That was my motto. No doubt, no uncertainty, no hesitation. Nobody believed doubters. Everybody believed believers. I dialed my father's number. It was going to be simple. I was going to ask to speak to him. Then I was going to say, "Dad, this is Jason."

A woman's voice said, "Good afternoon, this is Dr. Diaz's answering service. The office hours are Monday through Friday, nine to five. Is this an emergency?"

"Yes."

"Could you describe the problem?"

"I just want to speak to the doctor."

"I'm sorry, this is after office hours. If you describe your problem, Doctor will get back to you shortly."

I hung up. I stood there for a moment, then dialed the other Walcott Street number. "Hello," someone said. It sounded like a girl.

"Who's this?" I said.

"What? Who's this?"

"It's Jason," I said. A weird thought flashed through my mind. What if there was another Jason? What if he'd come home already?

"Jason Marks! Is that you again? What do you want this time, the math homework? Don't you ever do your own work?"

"Who is this?" I said.

"This is Miller Diaz, you fool. Don't you even know who you're calling? Is this Jason Marks or not?"

"It's Jason," I said.

"Oh, you are a fool. I'm sick of doing your homework for you." She hung up.

9

WHEN HER MOTHER called on Saturday, Miller was watering her plants. "Mom," she said, "how was your gig last night?"

"Good. A really responsive audience. What kind of a day are you having? Did you speak to your father?"

"I saw him in the office this morning."

"Did you eat a good breakfast? I don't want you eating junk food."

"Mom! You don't have to tell me things like that!"

"I was thinking, maybe you should go stay with your father tonight. I don't like you staying alone."

"It's good for me to be alone. I like being alone." She loved it! She loved the independence. She loved not having anybody hovering over her.

"It's just one more night. I'm going out for brunch with Dad and you know who tomorrow. I'll be fine. I'll be right here when you come home," she said emphatically.

Her parents protected her—overprotected her. But it wasn't all one way. She protected them, too. When something awful had happened in your family you couldn't just be a child anymore. You couldn't just *be*. You had to think. You didn't want to get too loud and you never let yourself get too angry. You tried to be happy, so your parents would feel good. You knew it wasn't your fault that your brother disappeared, but sometimes you felt like you were born to take his place, and you worried that you weren't doing too good a job of it.

"Anybody call?" her mother asked.

"No, just Ja—" Miller stopped herself. The call from Jason Marks had been bothering her—the way he'd asked her who she was and hadn't said his last name. He knew who she was! Anyway, just hearing the name Jason could get her mother upset. "Jason?" she'd say in that special voice, her anxious voice. "Oh, no. Not that again."

And then Miller would have to say, "Mom, it wasn't one of those calls."

The creep calls: Every time the newspaper ran an article about their family, and how many years had passed and no clues, and the family still waiting, there would be a rash of phone calls. It was like a sickness. All the ghouls crawled out of their holes. "Hi, this is Jason. This is your long lost baby! Guess where I'm calling from? the cemetery!" Sometimes they said things like, "Come pick me up quick. I'm at the Queen's Bridge intersection. Hurry!" Or sometimes they'd just scream.

The calls disgusted Miller. These people didn't have the brains to think or the heart to feel. Every time it happened her mother was upset for days, even though she carried on and said it was nothing.

The phone rang again while Miller was in the bathroom. She raced back to her room, but before she got there, she heard the answering machine click on. "This is Jason again. I'd like to speak to Connie."

Miller grabbed the phone. "Hello? Who is this?"

"Jason. Who am I talking to?"

"Jason who? Did you call before?"

"Does Connie live there?"

"Who are you? What do you want? Get off the phone! I don't think this is the least bit funny. I despise people like you!" She would have said a lot more, but the phone went dead.

10

I HEARD THE shuffle of feet beneath me. I looked out the window and saw my father's car in the driveway. I went down the stairs. *Let there be no doubt.* I didn't let myself think or hesitate or wonder if this was the right moment or what I would say. Enough time had passed. I'd been here too long already. All day yesterday, I'd been trying to get my nerve up. I didn't want to be out on the streets wandering around. I wanted to be in my parents' house. Three nights I'd slept in the garage and nothing had changed.

I heard my father downstairs and I went down. *Let there be no doubt.* Yes. It was now or never. Boom or bust. It was now, it was this moment, this place, these steps. One . . . two . . . I counted as I went down. *Let there be no doubt.*

My father was standing at the workbench. He didn't see me at first. Then he looked up and saw me. I was on the stairs. I could hear my breath, could feel the air being sucked up into my lungs, then rushing out.

"Hey!" my father shouted. "Who are you? What are you doing in my barn?"

"I'm Jason," I said.

"Jason who?"

"Jason, Jason Diaz."

His face went flat as a TV screen that had suddenly gone blank.

"Who are you?" he said. "What are you talking about?" He moved back away from me. "Where did you come from?"

"I'm your son. I've come home."

"The hell you are."

"I'm Jason," I said. I was scared. "I'm Jason. I'm your son."

This wasn't the way I had imagined it. This wasn't the way it was supposed to be. I thought my father would know me. He would pound his fist down. He would explode. He wouldn't let anything stand between us. He'd grab me so fast I wouldn't be able to breathe. He'd hold me so hard, nothing could ever separate us again.

"Who are you?" he said again. He said it carefully like he was feeling along the edge of a sore tooth.

"Jason."

"I have a son, Jason."

"Me."

"I'll say this for you, you've got nerve. What's the story?"

I STARTED TOWARD HIM. "I haven't got a story."

"Hold it right there." He had his hand up. "You stay right there. Now, I want the truth. What are you doing here? Where did you come from? Who are you? How did you find us?" Question after question.

"You're not letting me explain anything. You're not a very patient man," I said.

"I don't have time for this sort of thing. Who told you to say you were Jason? How did you find where we live?"

"The phone book."

He laughed. "Of course. Nothing to it. So what's your name?"

"Jason Diaz." I had my hand to my chest like I was pledging allegiance, but underneath my heart was going a mile a minute. "Jason Diaz," I said.

He picked up a hammer. "Now tell me your real name."

"Jas—" I was watching the hammer.

He tossed it aside. "I want the name you grew up with. The name you go by."

"Eddie. Eddie Leonard." It sounded wrong. It sounded like I'd just said a lie. "A lot of people call me Eddie Leonard, but I'm really Jason Diaz."

"Okay, Eddie, that's better." My father seemed to ease up, his face relaxed. He smiled. "Eddie, I could call the police. Do you want me to call the police, Eddie?"

I shrugged.

"I don't want to scare you, Eddie. Are you scared?"

He was toying with me, playing cat and mouse. Every time he said Eddie I flinched. My name is Jason I said to myself. Jason. I had nothing to hide Jason wouldn't be scared talking to his father. I wasn't scared. Jason wouldn't be standing stiffly. I leaned back against the wall. I had nothing to be afraid of. I was home, talking to my father.

He noticed that I was shivering. "You're scared. I'm not surprised. I'd be scared if I were in your shoes. It's hard to tell a lie."

"I'm not scared and I'm not lying. I'm Jason. I'm your son."

He looked at me for a moment and then he said, "Come on." He motioned me to go out of the garage ahead of him, then directed me to the house, and through a side door. We went up a short flight of stairs and into his office. "Sit there," he said, pointing to a leather couch.

He shut the door and sat behind his desk. His hand rested on the telephone. He was looking at me and not saying anything. I told myself not to say anything, either. I'd said enough. I looked around the room, at the plaster sets of teeth on the desk, and the framed diplomas on the wall behind him. "It's nice here," I said.

I didn't want to act nervous. I didn't want to act like I didn't know. *Let there be no doubt.* I could feel a twitch starting in one eye. I wanted a cigarette. I wanted to lean back, a cigarette caught between my fingers and let the smoke drift up toward the ceiling.

"Tell me, Eddie, how did you find us?"

"I told you, the telephone book."

"And you came from where?"

I mentioned the city.

"So how'd you find out about us?"

"I saw my picture on a wall."

"A missing child poster?" He showed me a framed picture on his desk. "This one?"

"Yes."

"You saw this picture and you recognized yourself?"

"Yes."

"Did you ever see the picture before?"

"No."

"But you knew it was you."

"Yes."

"And it convinced you, you were my son."

"Yes."

"I'll say this for you, you really don't have much of a story if that's the story you expect me to swallow. How did you get here? Where did you get the money?"

"I hitched. I got rides with people."

"And you figured you'd show up and we'd welcome you with open arms?"

"Yes. Maybe. Yes! I'm your son."

"I don't know if you're smart or stupid. I admire your nerve."

"Have you got a cigarette?" I said.

"I don't smoke and you shouldn't either. I don't know what your game is, Eddie. I've been looking for my son for a long time. People call, they say they've seen my son. I go check out their stories. I follow up on things. I don't give up easily. Each time I want it to be my son. You're the boldest one. You're the first one who's come to my door."

"That's because I'm Jason." I took the picture from the desk and held it up alongside my face. "See."

"Maybe you think there's money. People hear about a reward. Is that why you're here? You think you'll get money?"

I felt tired. I really wished I had a cigarette. There wasn't even an ashtray in the room.

He held a metal dental instrument and turned it between his fingers. It had a long probing tip and I thought about what he did, the way he poked into people's teeth. "Do you like the work you do?" I asked.

"How long have you been here, Eddie?"

"What do you mean? Here in town? I just got here."

"When?"

"I came Thursday night."

"It's Sunday. Where have you been staying since then?"

"Out there." I motioned to the garage.

"You mean you've been snooping around this house all this time? I'm going to call the police!"

"Go on," I said. "Call them if you want to. I wasn't snooping. I'm not a snoop. I'm your son, that's why I'm here." I fumbled around in my pockets. Nothing but loose change. Even a piece of gum would have helped. "I had to sleep someplace, didn't I? I didn't do anything to your property. I just used the rug to keep warm."

"Okay, Eddie, calm down, take it easy. Tell me something about your life." He leaned back in his chair. "Where do you live? Who do you live with? Where's your mother?"

"She's not my mother."

"What does that mean?"

"Jason Diaz has a mother, but not Eddie Leonard."

"I don't get it."

"I never saw her."

"You never saw your mother? Who brought you up? Your father?"

I shook my head. "I never saw him, either."

"Who do you live with?"

"My grandmother."

"And her name is Leonard? What did she tell you about yourself?"

"She told me a lot of things. She said Sharon brought me home and left me."

"Sharon?"

"Her daughter."

"You mean your mother."

"No, she was my grandmother's daughter. She said she found me in the back of a cab. I was wrapped in a blanket. She said I had a stuffed animal I wouldn't let go of."

"What kind of animal?"

"A dog with one ear."

He wrote something down. "Let me get this straight. Sharon, your grandmother's daughter, found you in a cab. Somebody else had left you there and she found you. What did the cabdriver say?"

"She was the cabdriver."

He swung around on the chair. "Quite a story," he said. "Didn't she remember who left you there?"

"No. She didn't know I was there till I started to cry."

"Why didn't she go to the authorities? If you didn't belong to her, why did she keep you?"

"She didn't. She brought me to my grandmother. My grandmother never believed Sharon's story. She said I was Sharon's kid and she kept me because she thought Sharon would come and get me someday."

"Where's Sharon now?"

"I don't know."

"When's the last time you saw your mother?"

"You mean Sharon? I never saw her."

"And your grandmother—where's she now?"

"She died last month."

"Who else is in your family?"

"My uncle Stew."

"So where is he?"

"In Florida, I guess."

"Have you got an address?"

"No."

"When was the last time you saw him?"

"About four years ago."

"So you don't have anyone?"

"No."

"Okay, it's a sad story, but why us?"

"Because I'm Jason."

"No good, Eddie. As a Jason story this rates a D or a zero or whatever the fail mark is. I've heard better stories from kindergarten kids."

The phone rang. He put his hand on the receiver, but didn't pick it up.

"I'm Jason," I said. I crossed my legs and put my foot up on my knee.

"You can say that until the cows come home. Why should I believe you? I look at you, I don't see my son, Jason. I listen to you, I don't hear my son, Jason."

The phone continued to ring. He finally picked it up. "Miller? Where are you, sweetie? . . . Good . . . Me, too. We'll be going in a few minutes. We're meeting Mary Anne." He listened for a minute. "Okay, sure, take Graham out for a run first." He hung up. "Listen," he said to me, "I don't want to be cruel, but maybe you should go to the Salvation Army. They can help you."

"I'm Jason, I'm Jason! I know I am." I stood up.

"Yes, you keep saying it. I wish it were true. And I don't believe you." He came around his desk and opened the door. "Come on," he said.

I followed him to the door. I was shaking. I was remembering all the times I'd come home and my grandmother had locked the door and there were no lights. "Where's my mother?" I said. "I want to talk to my mother."

He had the outside door open.

"You shouldn't be sending me away. You're going to be sorry."

I don't know if he pushed me or I slipped. I was on the steps and then I was down. When I tried to stand up, I couldn't.

"Stand up," he said.

I tried, but it hurt too much.

"Stand up!"

"I can't. I think I broke something."

11

MILLER KNEW THERE was something wrong the moment she got back from taking Graham for his run. The front door was standing open. Graham ran ahead of her into her father's offices. "Dad?" Miller called. He was in one of his operating rooms, bending over a boy sitting in a dental chair. She thought dental emergency at first, but he wasn't working on the boy's teeth. He was bandaging his ankle.

"Hey, man, that hurts," the boy said, as her father tightened the bandage. The boy was really cute. He had glossy black hair and high cheekbones.

"Don't be a baby," her father said to him. "Come here, Miller. Look at him. Look carefully. Does he look familiar? Anybody you know?"

Was it a joke? She didn't think so, not the way they both were waiting for her reaction. The boy was staring at her.

"I'm surprised you don't recognize him," her father said. He was definitely being ironic.

"Give me a clue."

"The first letter is J."

"Jason," the boy said.

"Jason!" her father said. "He says he's Jason. What do you think about that, Miller?"

She took a quick look at the boy. Now she was scared. Her brother? This was what she'd been waiting for all her life, but it didn't seem right that it was happening here, now, in her father's office.

Graham circled the room. He went up to her father for a pat, then sniffed the boy. The boy put his hand out.

Sometimes at night, if Miller couldn't sleep, she would imagine her brother in the shadows above the windows, and she'd talk to him. *Jason, when are you coming back? I never met you, but I miss you so much* . . . Talking to him, it was as if he was there, and it always made her feel better, stronger, and not so alone.

"He's Jason? Dad, that's not funny."

"You're right about that." Her father frowned angrily. "He thinks it's a joke to walk into people's lives and say anything that he damn pleases."

"I'm Jason," the boy said.

"You've said it ten times. You can say it a hundred times. And I still don't believe you, Eddie. His name is Eddie Leonard, Miller. Empty your pockets," he said suddenly to the boy. "Everything. I want to see everything. Turn your pockets out."

Miller couldn't believe how rough her father was and how the boy did everything he said. He let change and folded bills fall to the floor.

"No wallet?" her father said. "Don't you have a social security number? A driver's license?" He picked up a white card. "What's this? Where did you get this?"

"It's my library card," the boy said.

"Who gave you this card?" Now her father really sounded

mad. "Jason Diaz? Who gave you the right to use that name!"

"I did."

"You did. You did! I can't believe this. You can't put down any name you want to. That's my son's name."

"I'm Jason," the boy said. "I know I am."

"You can know anything you want to. You can know you're president of the United States. You can know you're king of the universe. The funny farms are full of people like that."

"Dad . . ." Miller said. What if the boy was really Jason? What made her father so sure he wasn't?

The phone was ringing upstairs. Graham's ears twitched, and he looked up at her. Normally she would have run to answer it—it might be her mother—but she let it ring. She couldn't leave now. She was afraid that if she did, the boy would disappear, and she'd never know if he was Jason or not.

"Can you stand up?" her father said. "Let me see you put some weight on the foot now."

The boy slid to the edge of the chair. "Is this going to hurt? I don't like pain." He stepped gingerly on the bandaged foot, winced, and caught the edge of the chair for support.

"Stand right on it," her father said. "It's not that bad. You just twisted it."

"It's not your foot," the boy said. He tried to stand again, then sat back down and rubbed his ankle.

"Do you have relatives in town, Eddie?"

"Lots of them."

"Give me a phone number, a name. I'll call. Somebody's got to come and get you."

"I mean you, you're my relatives."

He said it so simply, it brought tears to Miller's eyes. Her tears confused her. She believed him—and didn't believe him. How could they tell? How could they know for sure? They couldn't accept him just because he said he was Jason. Her father was right, anybody could say it. But why would he say it, if it wasn't true?

"Can I stay here tonight?" the boy said. "I'll sleep in the garage. I won't bother you."

Miller looked at her father. "Can he, Dad?"

"This kid's been sleeping out there since Thursday night."

Miller looked at the boy. "Thursday night? Did you close the doors?"

He nodded.

It was creepy. If he was who he said he was, why hadn't he come and knocked on the door? It made her think her father was right. The boy had made up this whole story so they'd take him in.

"I have proof," the boy said, reaching in his shirt pocket and taking out a folded sheet of paper.

It was a copy of the picture of Jason they had on the wall upstairs.

"It's Jason," Miller said.

"Miller, it's the picture we gave them to print. Do you know how many people have seen this picture? Anybody can get their hands on this picture. Come on," he said to the boy. "I'm taking you to the Salvation Army. They'll give you a bed for the night."

"Dad . . ." Her father was right, but still, what if it was Jason and they drove him away and they never saw him again?

The phone rang. Her father pushed a button. "Hello? Dr. Diaz's office."

"Bruce," her mother's voice came over the speaker. "It's

Connie. I've been ringing upstairs and Miller doesn't answer. Is she with you?"

"I'm right here, Mom," Miller said, talking over her father's shoulder. "And Mom, are you listening? There's a boy here who says he's Jason."

"What?"

"Yeah, we got a castaway, Connie," her father said. "Somebody here who's a dreamer or a leech—"

"What does he say? Where did he come from?"

"It's nothing, Connie. Don't even think of getting your hopes up."

"I want to talk to him."

"Mom!" Miller said. "I don't think he should just go. Dad wants to bring him down to the Salvation Army."

"Connie, I'm telling you, it's nothing."

"Wait, wait. I can't sort this out over the phone. I'll be home tonight. Bruce, keep him there."

"Connie—"

"Bruce, I can't talk about it now. I want to talk to him myself. I have to see him." She hung up.

Miller glanced at the boy. She had imagined Jason so many times, but she had never imagined this boy. She had felt she would know her brother the moment she saw him. There would be no question. And now here he was. And she didn't know him. He was sitting there with all this fuss going on around him, and he wasn't embarrassed or uncomfortable or anything. He just sat there waiting for whatever was going to happen, to happen.

12

MY FATHER TOSSED me a tie he took from the closet in his office. The tie looked like a rope and for a moment I couldn't figure out what it was for.

"Put the tie on, we're going out to eat breakfast," my father said.

"Brunch, Dad," my sister said.

"I don't wear ties," I said.

"You do when you're out with me. Comb your hair. We're going to the club."

I wound the tie around my neck like a bandage. I wanted to make my father laugh so he'd relax and like having me around. Uncle Stew would laugh if he saw me with this tie around my neck. Mind your manners! he'd mock, because he knew I didn't have any.

My father unwound the tie and tied it correctly. "You wear a tie when you go to the club."

"The boring country club," Miller said.

Everything I knew about country clubs came from the movies. Rich people went to country clubs. "I don't want to go there," I said. "I'll stay here. You can come back for me later."

"Don't even think it," my father said.

"Don't you trust me?" Did he think I was here for his money?

"You guessed right," my father said, as we went out to the car. "Connie says she wants to see you, and I'm not letting you out of my sight till she does. Let her figure out what to do with you."

In the car I sat in back. I propped up my bad foot and leaned back against the leather seats. My ankle ached, but I felt great. I was here! I kept nudging myself, because it was like a dream. Here we were, my father, my sister, and me, together in my father's car. It was mellow. There were so many things I wanted to know. I had ten times as many questions to ask him as he had asked me. Start with cars. Did he like to drive? How many different cars had he had? Was this his favorite? Would he let me drive it sometimes?

And there were things I wanted to know about my sister, Like how old she was and what grade she was in. "What's the name of your school?" I said.

Miller put her hand back and made a circle with her fingers.

"O what?" I said.

"Osborne."

"High school?"

She shook her head. I liked her tiny ears. She wore pink plastic earrings, one side a puppy, the other side a kitten.

"What grade?" I touched one of her earrings.

Her head snapped around. "What are you doing?" She felt one earring and then the other, like I was trying to take them from her. She turned to look at me. "What are you staring at?"

"You. I can't believe you're my sister."

She turned around and didn't say anything.

It was like a slap in the face. It was like a bomb exploding. I felt like I was moving through a mine field. I didn't know what was going to explode next.

At the country club my father motioned me out of the car then went on ahead. I had trouble walking and Miller gave me her shoulder. Just that little thing—my hand on her shoulder—made me feel good again. She likes me, I thought. I'm going to make my father like me, too.

A woman sitting at a table, waved. "Mary Anne's here," Miller said.

"Who's that?"

"My stepmother."

It took me a moment to get it. "He and Connie don't live together?"

"My parents are divorced," she said.

Her parents. I heard that.

"Are you surprised?"

"Everything here is a surprise."

"What did you expect?"

"You know, I thought we'd all be together."

But then we were at the table. "Mary Anne, this is Jason," Miller said.

"His name is Eddie," my father said.

Mary Anne gave me a smile. "Sit down," she said.

The waitress came over. "How are you today, Dr. Diaz?" She noticed my foot up on a chair. "You're lucky you have Dr. Diaz to take care of you."

After we ate our pancakes, my father and Mary Anne went over to talk to a couple at another table. I moved my chair closer to Miller's. "Do you come here a lot?"

"Not a lot. Mostly when Mom's away."

"Why is she away?"

"Mom's a musician and she plays in a band and writes music."

"Are you good at music, too?" I said.

"Nothing special." She frowned. She had nice eyebrows, dark like mine. "I'm probably more like Dad, a science type."

Who was I like? I had never thought of myself as a science type. "I like music," I said and started drumming on the table. "I like to sing, too."

"Do you like Mary Anne?" Miller said suddenly.

"She's okay. I don't like her and I don't dislike her. I like Connie better."

"How can you say that? You haven't even seen her yet."

"My own mother? I saw her before you did. Anyway, I don't have to see her to know I like her better."

Miller nodded, as if what I said made sense—and it did, but I felt uneasy. What was my mother going to say when she saw me? Would she know me, or would she be influenced by my father? I glanced over at him and Mary Anne. What had he told her about me? That I was just a nervy kid trying to freeload on the family.

When they came back my father checked out my empty plate. "The food's great," I said.

"When's the last time you had a meal this good?" my father said.

"My grandmother was a good cook." I had to laugh. My grandmother almost never cooked. We ate from cans and soggy take-out cartons. Sometimes I thought she fed me from the same cans she fed the cat from. But I sure wasn't going to say that. "She could make anything," I said. "She made tuna fish salad, potato salad, macaroni salad, spaghetti, all kinds of spaghetti. My grandmother—"

"I thought she wasn't your grandmother," my father said.

"She wasn't."

"So why do you call her your grandmother?"

"I guess I could call her Lorraine."

And then the questions started again. "Where did you say you lived? What was your house like? Do you have friends?"

"Three best friends," I said. That was true, but saying I lived in the nicest house on the block wasn't exactly accurate, but it made a better impression. "We had a garden in back."

Bruce stirred his coffee. "A garden? Who took care of it? I thought you said your grandmother was sick."

"A man came twice a week." A man had made a garden behind the house, but it had nothing to do with us.

My father had me repeat my address and my grandmother's name. He wrote it down. "And your mother, the woman who brought you to her, your grandmother's daughter, did she come to see you a lot?"

"She never came to see me."

"Why do you think that was?"

"I didn't think anything. I was a kid. I waited."

"And your father?" I knew he was weighing everything I said, trying to catch me in a trap with my own words.

"He never came," I said. "I had no father." I looked down, then took a sip of water. I forced back the sadness that rose in my throat. It took a moment before I could risk looking into his face. I waited for him to say something, something about him and me, even just that he was glad I was here. But he didn't. Instead he raised his hand and called for more coffee.

13 My FATHER HAD A house in the hills just outside of town. It was like a ranch with barns and a corral and a horse for everyone in the family. A white Arabian for Mary Anne, a black horse for my father, and a tan one for Miller. Even Feenee, Mary Anne's little girl, who was like a color copy of Mary Anne, had a pony of her own. The only one who didn't have a horse was Nathan, the baby. I went crazy thinking that someday maybe I'd have a horse of my own, too.

I lilp-hopped after Miller as she groomed her horse. My foot was aching, and I put it up on a bale of hay to take the weight off it. I could hear the horses on the other side of the partition, chewing and moving restlessly. "This is the life," I said to Miller.

Bruce came out. He'd changed into jeans and rubber boots. Two German shepherds were with him, Princess was the mother and the smarter of the two. Boy kept going up to my father and begging him to play. My father roughed him up a little. "Boy, you are some kind of pest." Each time he said it I made believe it was me he was talking to. Talking rough, but underneath telling me he really liked me.

He and Miller mucked out the stalls and fed the horses. I tried to help, but my father said, "Sit down and stay out of the way."

Boy brought me a ball. I threw it and he fetched it. The bad feelings started coming back. I was here, I'd come home, I was in my father's house, but it was like . . . nothing. Nobody acted like it was anything special.

Miller saddled up her horse and went down the road with the dogs. She didn't ask if I wanted to ride. I'd never ridden a horse in my life but I was willing to try.

Later my father drove Miller and me back to their house on Walcott Street to wait for my mother. On the way we stopped and had a pizza. My father started quizzing me again. "How're you in school? Do you like it? What's your favorite subject?"

"All my teachers want me to go to college."

Bruce nodded. He was tipped back on his chair.

"I'm thinking about computers," I said. "Or maybe something in television." I took a sip of soda. "One of my teachers told me I had a good broadcasting voice."

"You have a nice voice." Miller nibbled the crust from the pizza.

What the gym teacher had told me, in fact, was that I had a big mouth and if I didn't shut it, he'd throw me out of class. I swished the Coke around in the can. The more I talked, the more I made up. It was like kicking holes in the bottom of a boat. I was sinking myself. I knew Bruce wasn't being taken in. I wasn't getting anything past him. One of these times he was going to nail me. And then what? Then I'd say, *Yes, I told a few stories. I wanted to make a good impression on you, so you'd think well of me.*

That at least was the truth.

"How's your writing?" he asked me.

"Good. My teacher always read my compositions in front of the class, then put them up on the wall. My writing got a special award from Mr. Babka, the assistant principal."

That had been when my grandmother was sick and I'd been missing school a lot. One day Mr. Babka called me to his office and showed me one of the excuses I'd written. *Please excuse my grandsons unfortunate absense from school. Unfortunately he has had many family obligasions. Unfortunately I have not been well.* Unfortunate had been one of my favorite words.

"This is a finely written document," Mr. Babka said. "Very touching. You get an A for imagination, a D for spelling, and F for skipping school. Keep it up, Eddie, and I predict that you will never graduate. And that's unfortunate."

It was dark when we got to the house. "Connie's not here yet?" Bruce said. He sounded annoyed.

We waited downstairs in the kitchen. Bruce kept going out and doing things and coming back and checking his watch. I sat by the window. I could see the garage where I'd slept and the trees I'd come through. I tried not to think about my mother, what she would say, what I would say. I was just waiting for the moment when she would come in. It could be right. It could be wrong. It could all be over in a second.

In the glass I saw the reflection of the room behind me. I saw my father and Miller. It was unreal. It was as if I was alone and had made this whole thing up—this house, these people . . . I was afraid if I turned too quickly, there would be nobody there.

My father came over and stood by the window next to me. I wanted to touch him. I wanted him to put his arm around me. I wanted to say *Dad,* and then I said it. "Dad—"

He looked at me and shook his head. "What time did she say she'd be home, Miller?" He was looking at his watch again.

MILLER WAS THE FIRST to notice the headlights in the driveway. She ran out. Graham followed her barking. I heard her say, "Mom!"

I thought I was prepared. I thought I was cool. This was what I'd been waiting for, but the moment I heard Miller say *Mom,* I went rigid. I heard her come in. My back was to her. I knew I should turn around, but I couldn't. I felt her looking at me, and the hairs on the back of my neck stood up.

"Hello."

I turned and gripped the back of a chair.

She took off her coat. "Sorry you had to wait for me. Our plane was late." She stood there with her arm around Miller. She was tall, as tall as I was.

"We were in a holding pattern for half an hour. The whole weekend was like that. Waiting for things to start."

She sat down at the table.

I couldn't stop looking at her. "You play in a band," I said. I said the first stupid thing that came to my head. I hopped up on my good leg, then went lurching across the room. "Hi, Mom," I yelled. "It's me. I'm home."

"Sit down, sit down, please," she said. "Sit down, you don't have to stand."

I kept smiling. I couldn't stop myself. I wanted everything to happen fast, that second. I thought if I kept smiling, everything would go the way I wanted it to.

"So . . . ?" she said, looking at my father.

He shrugged. "There he is."

My mother sighed. Her eyes, which had been so large and

bright when she came in, looked tired now. I could feel my own face falling. "We've been talking," I said. "Haven't we, Dad? Having a good time, getting to know each other. I was at the country club and at the ranch—"

"What's with the foot?" she said.

"Oh, nothing. Just a little accident."

"Fortunate accident for him," my father said.

"Bruce," my mother said.

"Okay, Connie. I talked to him. Wait until you talk to him."

My foot started to really hurt. I sat down and put it up. I kept hearing my uncle Stew's voice. *Fool, they're going to kick your ass out of their house. . . .* "Hey, Mom and Dad," I said. "I'm home!" *But nobody cheered.*

14

I LOOKED AT CONNIE. I looked at Bruce. Connie and Bruce. My parents. All day I had been trying to convince myself that I was who I said I was and thought I was, but . . . why didn't they know me? There must be something of Jason left in me. They should have seen something.

"What do you think?" my father said to Connie. What he meant was, What do you think about *him*? Me. "Am I right or not?" He rocked on his heels, hands in his back pockets.

"I don't know," My mother rubbed her eyes. "I can't think about it right now, Bruce. I'm too tired and it's too late. I'll talk to him tomorrow morning."

"And—?"

"And, I don't know! Don't rush me."

"Suit yourself." He spun around.

That was weird! It was the same way I used to spin and drive my grandmother crazy. I must have gotten that spinning stuff from him.

"All I want to know is what do we do *now*," Bruce said to Connie, "while you're making up your mind? He's here.

Where does he stay? Do you want me to take him to the Y or do I have to take him back with me to the ranch?"

"He can stay right here."

"Are you serious? I don't want him in the house."

"I don't have your fears, Bruce."

"Connie, use your head." He took her by the arm and whispered in her ear.

I caught a word here and there. Bruce was telling her that she didn't know me. I could be a thief, a rapist, a crackhead. He kept talking, and she kept looking at me and shaking her head. "No," she said finally. "No. End of discussion. He's staying."

"In the garage."

"He's not staying in the garage."

"I don't mind," I said.

They both looked at me.

Bruce was right to be suspicious. He was tough, and that was the way a father should be.

"I'll go to the garage," I said. "Dad's right. You shouldn't let me stay in the house until you're positive about me."

Connie let out a snort. "You don't trust yourself?"

"I do, but I want you to trust me, too. I want you to be sure." She laughed, and it was beautiful the way her face opened up. She was a beautiful person.

When Bruce left, Connie went upstairs with me and showed me where I was going to sleep. It was a room next to hers, with a bed and a bureau and not much else except a teddy bear in a rocking chair by the window. Connie didn't say it, but I guessed it was Jason's room. My old room.

I lay in the dark, awake. My foot ached. Cars passed outside, tires crackled on the pavement. Light fell across the walls, and they lightened and darkened. At moments the room turned red. *The red room* . . . Images streamed through my head. I couldn't sleep. So much had happened; it didn't seem possible that I was in my parents' house, in the room I'd once slept in, maybe in the same bed. Everything had happened so fast, so simply, like stepping from one room into another. Four days ago I was in my grandmother's apartment, in another life.

Where would I be tomorrow? I felt as if I were on a slowly moving train. Even as I lay here I was being carried along. There still was time to get off, but the train was beginning to pick up speed. Tomorrow might be too late.

There was a constant ping and crackle of heat from the walls, as if there was something unsettled and stirring in the room. Every time a car passed the teddy bear's yellow eyes lit up, and it glared at me. My eyes moved left and right and up across the ceiling, corner to corner, almost as if they had found and fallen into an old familiar groove. Was this where my bed had been, the wall against my left cheek, the long square of the window above me? The window, the cold glass . . . I remembered cold rooms. I remembered families I'd stayed with, hours I'd spent alone locked in dark rooms, standing by the window, pressed against the cold glass, arms outstretched, waiting for feathers to sprout so I could fly away.

IN THE MIDDLE OF the night I came awake. For a second I thought I was Eddie Leonard again, back on 28th Street hearing the traffic that never ended. I heard an explosion, but it was only the backfire of a passing truck. I was restless. My ankle burned every time I turned. I finally got out of bed and went looking for aspirin. Each step sent shooting pains up my leg. In the bathroom, I took two aspirin with water.

My crazy face stared back at me from the mirror. Hair

stuck against my face, squinty eyes, one swollen red ear sticking out like a fungus. That face! Connie should never have let me stay in her house. Urrrgh! I wanted to scare them, make them pay attention. I wanted their eyes to pop open. I wanted to hear them scream, *Jason, Jason, Jason!*

Graham came to investigate. He poked into me. I pushed my face deep into his hairy coat listening to the beat of his dumb heart. Why didn't they love and trust me the way they loved and trusted their dog? I'd be their dog. I'd run, I'd fetch, I'd wag my tail.

I WENT DOWN TO the kitchen. I fed Graham and made myself a sandwich. I stood and read the notes on the refrigerator. There were clippings, stuff about diet and nutrition, and some back and forth notes. *"Mom! I wore your silver earrings. They were perfect." "Millie luv, meat loaf wrapped in silver foil. If Amy calls, tell her lesson is on."*

I found a pen in a drawer and scribbled my own note. *"It's good to be home, Mom, Millie, and Dad, too. I love you all. Jason."*

15

IN THE MORNING I heard voices downstairs. Connie's voice. *Not Connie,* I told myself. *My mother. My mother, my mother, my mother!* I hopped down the stairs. My mother was waiting for me. There were so many things I wanted to ask her. She'd want to ask me things, too. She'd want to know about Eddie Leonard—the nonyears, the years of the no life of Jason Diaz.

It was dark on the stairs and light in the kitchen. I felt like I was coming from the darkness of my nonlife to the light of my real life.

My mother was sitting in the window seat that looked out to the trees in back. She wore jeans and a pullover covered with stars and comets. She was smoking a cigarette. I stood in the doorway looking at her. I couldn't stop looking at her. She was beautiful. She was my mother. My mother was sitting there by the window. I kept saying it to myself, hammering it into my head. I was ready to explode I was so glad.

"Good morning," she said. She sort of waved her cigarette

at me. There was a halo of smoke over her head. "Help yourself. Milk's in the fridge, cereal's on the table."

"The sun's shining," I said. "This is a really fantastic day! This is the greatest day of my life."

She didn't say anything. She just sat there. What did she think, that I was just a crazy kid off the streets? I poured cereal into a bowl, then hopped over to the refrigerator and got the milk. I ate a spoonful of cornflakes. Milk dribbled down my chin. *Idiot, don't eat now!* I pushed the bowl away and wiped my mouth. "Where's Miller?"

"Gone to school. How's your foot?"

"Okay." She kept flicking the cigarette into a saucer. Boy, was I nervous. I pointed to the pack of cigarettes. "Can I have one?"

"A cigarette? You smoke?"

"Sometimes."

"If you were my son . . ." She stopped.

"I am your son." I looked at her expectantly. "That's the point. That's why I'm here."

She got up and put out her cigarette in the sink. "I don't allow smoking in my house."

"You're smoking."

She dropped the butt into a wastebasket. "I've quit a thousand times. It's a killer trying to break this habit. You don't want to get started. You're too young to smoke."

"I don't, that much." Why were we talking about cigarettes? "It's just when I'm tense."

"What are you tense about?"

She had to be kidding. I pointed to her. "You know. Us."

She played with the pack of cigarettes, then dropped them into the garbage. "How long have you been smoking?"

"Since I was eight years old."

"Eight years old!"

"My uncle gave me my first cigarette. Uncle Stew. He's not my real uncle. He's my grandmother's son."

"I never thought you'd be a smoker."

"If you don't want me to smoke, I quit."

"I didn't know I had that influence."

"You do. You're my mother."

She wiped the counter, shut a cupboard door, then came over and sat near me. "Go on," she said.

"Go on? I'm Jason," I said. "I've come home."

"I don't know."

I waited.

"I don't know you," she said. "You just walk in here and . . . I don't know what's in your mind. You're not my little boy. I've had my hopes up so many times, I've had so many false leads, I've let myself believe . . ."

"I'm Jason. You can believe me."

"I want you to be Jason."

"I'm Jason," I said again. *Let there be no doubt.*

"Maybe you are. Maybe you're not. I have to find out."

I nodded. I said, "I understand." I kept thinking about a cigarette. "I'm Jason," I said. How many times had I said it now? "Jason," I said.

"Jason," she said. She said it softly. "Jason." She closed her eyes.

"Do you believe me?"

"I believe that you believe what you're saying."

"Does that mean—"

"It means whatever you want it to mean. It means . . . I don't know what I mean." She sighed. "I look at you and I want it to be you . . ." She got bread from the cupboard and put a slice in the toaster.

"Jason," she said, "Eddie, or whoever you are, I don't

know if you can understand this, but I'm so scared I can hardly think straight."

She sat down opposite me again. "On the way home last night I was afraid you'd be gone by the time I got here. Then when I saw you, I thought, Yes that could be Jason, but I didn't know."

"If you didn't know me, why did you let me stay?"

"Did you want me to say you've got five minutes to get out of my house?"

She gave me a kindly smile. I hated it. I didn't want her to be nice. I wanted her to know. "If I'm not Jason, why would I be here?"

"You're sure, aren't you? You know you're Jason."

She wanted me to say yes. I could tell she wanted me to *know*. "Don't you recognize me?" I said.

"I should know you, even after all these years." She studied my face. "What's that on your eyebrow? Is that a scar?"

I felt along my eye. "I guess so." I'd always had a faint white line there.

"Jason fell out of his high chair when he was a year old and split his eyebrow."

"He had a scar right there?"

It felt like her answer was a million years in coming.

"I thought it was the right eye," she said.

I felt the place. "No, it's the left eye."

It could have happened the way she said. I could have fallen out of my high chair. I was too young to remember that. But I did remember something—my grandmother getting mad at me once and throwing a glass that hit me in the face.

16 I LEANED OUT the window. The air was cool. The trees were full of the sound of birds. I knelt there the way I had when I was little, looking out at the trees. I loved it here, the cool, the green, the birds chattering. It sure wasn't 28th Street, with its parking lots and hot black roofs. This is perfect, I thought, this is what happiness is. This is where I belong.

It was my fourth day in the house. As soon as I thought that, I didn't feel so happy. Nothing was settled. My mother had said I could stay until my foot healed. And then what? Sometimes I thought she was really accepting me, but I didn't know. I couldn't tell about any of them. Even Bruce, who was tough, was different from day to day.

I heard them in the kitchen, and I went down. Connie was making Miller's lunch. Miller was eating cornflakes with milk, the same thing she ate every morning.

"You sure like cornflakes," I said, picking up the box. She grabbed it out of my hand. "Oh, your special cornflakes," I said. I was teasing, the way I'd seen brothers and sisters tease on TV.

"That's her favorite brand," my mother said. "She's liked those since she was a baby." I'd already heard her say it two or three times. She didn't have to leap to Miller's defense every minute. It was like telling me I was an outsider. *This is ours. These are the real Diazes' cornflakes.*

"Don't worry, I'm not going to eat Miller's special cornflakes." I patted Miller on the head.

"Mom! Will you tell him to back off?"

I put my hands up. "I'm backing off," I said. I didn't care about her ridiculous cornflakes. What I minded was that Connie, my mother, never defended me, never asked me anything about myself, never called me anything—not even Eddie. Sometimes she called me Graham's friend, because Graham hung around me so much. Maybe she thought I was Jason for one second a day. I propped my bum foot on a chair. The good mood I'd been in was gone. I felt crazy again. *I'm Jason. No, I'm not. I'm Eddie. . . . I'm Eddie. No, I'm not. I'm Jason . . .*

I was here. I was home. What did I have to do to convince them? The nights I'd slept in the garage I'd dreamed about my family snug in this house. It had been cold in the garage, but I had been warm in my heart thinking how we'd be together soon. *Nice dream, Eddie.*

My mother held up the bread. "Toast?"

I nodded.

"How about some eggs?"

"Mom," Miller said, "you're spoiling him."

"Not the way she spoils you."

Miller ignored me and got up. "I'm going, Mom. Are you going to be here when I come home?"

"I'll be here," I said.

She gave me a nasty look. I gave her a smile. "I can't help teasing you," I said. "I thought little sisters liked teasing." That fell flat, too.

"I've got lessons at the studio today," my mother said, "and this afternoon my group is getting together, but I should be back by supper, Miller."

After Miller left, the two of us were alone. Time to talk, but what did we talk about? "How's the foot?" she said. "We want that foot to heal."

My foot, yes. The big subject. "It's getting better." I stood up to show her. I was sick of my foot. "I never knew a musician," I said.

"Now you do."

"I mean, a real live one."

"Real people make music."

"I know, but I never thought I'd have a mother who played the trumpet." It was her chance to say: Now you do.

"If a day passes and I'm not at the piano or holding the horn, I don't feel alive," she said.

Then there was one of those long silences. She was looking at me, studying me. I could almost hear the wheels turning. *Is he . . . maybe . . . no . . . yes . . . yes, he might be . . .* She had her head tilted to one side, and she was giving me a really warm look, one of those *Yes he is* looks. Then she got up and cleared the table, wiping it, as if it was the most important thing in the world.

I said, "Remember what you said? You said you'd been disappointed—"

"About what?"

I pointed to myself. "Me. Jason. About all the different Jasons. Did any of them ever come here and say they were me?"

"No."

"I'm the first? Nobody ever came in the house before?"

"No."

"Just me?"

"Yes."

"Okay!" I leaned back. "And you know why none of them ever came here? Because none of them was me!"

She laughed and rumpled my hair. "You're such a funny kid. What are you going to do today?"

"Wash the floor."

"I want you to stay off the foot."

"Don't worry, Mom!" I looked up at the clock. "You better go." We were doing it! We were being mother and son. I felt like jumping up and hugging her, but after she left, the bad thoughts rushed over me.

She doesn't want you. She doesn't know you. She doesn't care about you. She doesn't think you're her son. Remember what she said? Stay off the foot. She can't wait for your foot to heal, so she can get you out of her house.

"Come on, Eddie!" I said aloud. Graham looked up. I grabbed him by the muzzle and shook his head back and forth. "Let there be no doubt. She trusts you! That's why she leaves you here alone. That's trust!"

Graham broke free and started barking. He agreed.

I went around the house. I opened drawers, poked into closets, pulled boxes down from shelves. I found loose change and some bills. I found a pocketknife with a mother of pearl finish. I put it in my pocket. "That's trust," I said, but then I put it back.

I used to lift things from my grandmother. If she caught me I'd lie. "I never touched it! No! Not me, never!" I still got slugged. It got so I'd lie for the sake of lying, just to get back at her. But not here. Jason wouldn't take. Eddie would, but not Jason.

I fooled with the stereo equipment, banged the drums. There were gongs and flutes and different horns I blew into. I arranged the tapes on the shelves, made them neat.

I sat with a small set of drums between my knees. "Ja-son Di-az, Ja-son Di-az." I repeated it like a chant. "Ja-son Di-az, Ja-son Di-az," singing the words and feeling them bang through my fingers.

When I sang, "Ed-die Leon-ard," it sounded wrong. It was off-key. Eddie Leonard! I didn't recognize the name anymore. Get him out of this house! I slapped the drums again. There was no Eddie Leonard. "Ja-son Di-az . . . Ja-son Di-az . . ." I slapped them. Slap the drums, my skin against the drum's skin, skin to skin, the beat going from one hand to the other, left then right, then left again, wall to wall, floor to ceiling, door to window. *Ja-son Di-az, Ja-son Di-az.* The drums repeating it over and over . . .

I WENT DOWNSTAIRS to my father's office. Graham ran ahead and kept looking back as I hopped down the stairs. "Good morning, Father," I said to myself. "Good morning, son," I said back to me. My father was in one of the examining rooms bent over a patient. I leaned against the door and studied his face, looking to see if his attitude toward me had changed from yesterday. He glanced up, but he didn't say anything.

Later, I went into his office to bring him the paper. "Oh," he said. "You still here?"

"Like smelly cheese," I said. It was supposed to be a joke.

He glanced at the paper. "How's the foot?"

"Getting better."

I hung out in the office for a while, talking to the receptionist. The phone kept interrupting. Marjorie, one of the hygienists, came out to check the appointment book. She'd cut her hair since yesterday. "Nice haircut," I said.

"Do you think so?" She went back inside.

Roz handed a patient a form to fill out.

"Running behind?" I said.

"What else is new?"

The phone rang and she picked it up. The phone kept ringing, people kept coming and going. "Want me to do something?" I asked. She shook her head. I flipped through a magazine. I had this feeling . . . I don't know, like all this was mine. Maybe the people who worked for my father didn't know I was Jason yet. But then, maybe they all knew and were telling each other, but not in front of my father, who hadn't said anything yet. I'd tell them. You want to know something I'd say, I'm Jason Diaz. Doctor Diaz's son. I've been away, but I'm back now.

17

"A BOY IN YOUR HOUSE!" Francesca's eyes had doubled in size when Miller first told her.

"Not a boy," Miller said. "Maybe my brother."

"Maybe. But maybe a boy. And he's cute, right?"

"Very," Miller admitted.

"You're so lucky," Francesca said.

It was easy for Francesca to talk, but Miller had to live with him. It didn't seem like her house anymore. She had to be dressed when she left her room, and remember to lock the bathroom door. The toilet seat was always up. He never remembered to put it down. Even knowing that he'd been there before her made her feel, uuck!

Plus he was teaching Graham bad habits. He was always teasing and fighting with him and making Graham crazy. Plus he took stuff into his room that didn't belong to him, like her old stereo from the closet. Granted, nobody was using it, but who gave him permission? And why was she thinking about him? She couldn't even walk home from school with her own thoughts anymore.

Her mother was so trusting the way she left him alone in the house all day. Sure, her father was only a few steps away in his office, but he didn't know what was going on upstairs. None of them really knew. She had the feeling that he had poked through all their personal stuff. How had he found her old stereo if he hadn't been snooping where he didn't belong?

When she asked him about it, he said, "Do you want it back? I'll put it back if you want me to." That wasn't the point. She didn't want it. She had a CD player and a new stereo in her room that her aunt Lila had given her for her birthday. The point was, he didn't have a right to take what wasn't his without asking, and she said so. Then he apologized, but the look on his face said, *Little rich girl can't let go of anything.*

The whole thing stayed with her, like something unpleasant stuck in her throat, because if he was Jason, then she ought to be sharing with him. You shared with your brother, so why was she having these petty mean feelings? But the point of *that* was, How did she know he was her brother?

But why would he be here if he wasn't Jason?

"To worm his way into your family," Francesca said.

According to her, Miller was suffering from an acute stage of sibling jealousy. "Single children are always selfish and spoiled." Francesca could be so simplistic. "Look at us," Francesca said. "We're used to being the center of our parents' attention, or parent, in my case."

Miller conceded that maybe she was spoiled and wanted to be the star in her family, but she wanted her brother, too. Her real brother.

She really needed to talk to her mother about all this, but that was another thing—with him around, it was hard to get time alone with her mother these days. He was always there.

But that night, finally, she got her mother to herself. He'd gone to bed early. Her mother was in her bedroom sitting on the floor with her earphones on, listening to some tapes. Miller sat down near her. "Mom?" Her mother opened her eyes and smiled at her. Her mother's eyes could be so beautiful sometimes. "Am I bothering you?"

Her mother took off the earphones. "You always bother me, sweetie. No, you never bother me."

Miller knelt down close to her mother and whispered, "Is that boy Jason, Mom?"

Her mother got up to shut the door. "What do you think?"

"I guess he could be. But I think if he was really Jason, we'd be screaming with joy. We'd be jumping off the roof."

Her mother nodded. "I think you're right. We're too quiet. But I think he's Jason. Every day I think it more, but I'm not sure."

"I used to think when I was little that Jason was mad at us and had gone around the block to stay with a friend. Then I got older and kids teased me and said my brother was never coming back. I remember, once, someone telling me you can't hope forever. But people who say that don't know. You can hope forever. You do, don't you? You never stop waiting and hoping."

"He's a nice boy. I like him better each day."

"Mom, how are we going to know?"

"We will. I'll know what I feel, what my heart says."

Oh, great! Her mother's heart was just what Eddie was always working on. Like the other night when he'd sat with her and told her how, when he was little, his grandmother locked him in the house when she went to work and left him all day with a box of doughnuts and some Kool-Aid.

Granted, it was a sad story, but was it a true story? Sometimes the way Eddie said things Miller knew they were true —he'd had a hard life, a lot harder than hers—but other times, no, she didn't believe him.

"What I don't understand, Mom, is what's the point of him saying he's Jason, if he's not? What's he got to gain?"

"A home," her mother said.

"But what if he isn't Jason? We can't let him stay here! How are we going to know for sure? Don't we have to know?"

"Yes, but we have to give it time. Every day, it's getting clearer."

"Is it?" Miller said.

"I hope so. I have to believe that."

Eddie? Jason? When she thought about it afterwards, and how uncertain her mother was, Miller felt like she was picking petals from a daisy. Eddie? Jason? It was like putting on a glove, then taking it off. Jason. Eddie. Was he or wasn't he? Maybe he was Jason Eddie. Very funny, Miller.

What if it was a game he was playing, a bet he had with someone, or maybe he was wired up for some dumb TV show and they were being videotaped and everything they said and did was being recorded, so the whole country could laugh at this family that didn't know its own kid.

That was a cynical thought. Miller didn't think she was cynical, but she did like to think she had her eyes open. What she knew was that he—Eddie, Jason, the boy—had been in the house more than a week, and nothing was the way it had been before. Graham, who was her dog, was always with Eddie these days. And what did her father talk about now when she went in to see him? "How's Eddie? How's his foot? It's not going to heal if he jumps around on it all the time."

She was so bored with hearing about Eddie!

But there was no escape. When she went upstairs after school, he was there and giving her orders. "Don't walk on the bathroom floor yet."

"Why? What'd you do in there?"

"Very funny. I washed it."

Voluntarily, of course. It was to impress her mother. Miller went down to the kitchen, muttering to herself. He came clumping after her. "Watch where you step. I washed the kitchen floor, too."

"Hey, whose house is this, anyway?"

"Okay," he said smoothing his hair. He knew he was good looking. "That's interesting. Let's talk about it."

He always wanted to talk. Well, maybe she didn't. And she would like to eat without him watching her. She'd planned to come home and finish off the leftover chicken. She liked gnawing the bones, but not with him watching her get grease all over her fingers and mouth. She settled for a couple of chocolate fudge cookies and a glass of milk. She knew he was counting. She considered taking the cookie box upstairs and gorging in private.

"I've been waiting for you all day," he said. "You want to take a walk with me?" And he gave her a great smile. It made her feel that he thought she was terrific. And presto! she liked him again. She couldn't even stay mad at him.

They went out. He hip-hopped along, telling her some awful but sort of funny stories about his grandmother and his uncle Stew. They were a pair of monsters!

"Did Mom and Dad talk about me?" he asked.

"Who?" She still wasn't used to him saying Mom and Dad.

"Mom and Dad! Connie and Bruce. Did they talk about me after I was gone?"

"We always thought about Jason."

"What did they say?"

"Not a lot."

"So I went away and that was it," he said. "Bye-bye, baby. Were they happy to see me go?"

"No, that's stupid! They loved you."

"If they loved me why'd they let me go? Why didn't they get me back? They got you fast enough."

"What are you talking about? They didn't do it on purpose. Mom and Dad never stopped looking for you."

"So you do believe I'm your brother." He smiled triumphantly, as if he'd gotten her to admit something.

She didn't know how to tell him that when you grow up in a family where something awful has happened, you don't talk about it all the time. You don't have to talk about it. It's in your mind . . . and your mother's mind, and your father's mind. It's there all the time. You know it when your mother's eyes get too bright and she squeezes you too tight. And you know it when your father checks on you ten times an hour, when all you're doing is sitting in your room, playing.

She remembered the first time she heard the story of how Jason had disappeared. "Vanished from the face of the earth." That was the phrase Miller remembered. And for the longest time, she would walk along the street afraid that a hole would suddenly open in front of her and swallow her up, too.

"You don't know what it's like," she said.

"Oh, yes I do," he said, and became quiet.

That was the moment when she thought, Yes, maybe it was true. He was Jason, her brother. But she didn't say it, because she didn't completely believe it even then.

They walked all around the neighborhood, past the library and by the school, and she couldn't help it, she felt proud that she was with her brother. Every time they saw somebody she knew she sort of nodded or waved at them and she felt like yelling, Hi, this is my brother!

If he was her brother.

That's what she always got back to. Was he her brother? Or just a boy? And if he was just a boy, what kind of boy was he? "Sometimes I'd think of y—" She almost said *you*. "I'd think of what happened, and I'd cry just thinking about it. And then sometimes I'd think, Oh, my brother, he's having this wonderful life! And I'd envy him."

"Envy?" he said. "You envied me?"

"I'd think of you living with this big perfect family—"

"You're the one who had the perfect life!"

"—big perfect family in the country, with lots of brothers and sisters and dogs and cats and chickens and cows and horses. You'd all sit down together every day for breakfast and talk and pass the food and—"

"That's not the way I lived."

"I know! But I'm talking about what *I* thought. Don't be dense. I'm trying to tell you something. My life wasn't just perfect! I used to think that Mom and Dad looked at me and wished I was you. I used to think that when you came home, they wouldn't want me anymore, and they would send me away."

"Fat chance."

"Oh, they wanted you so much. You were beautiful, and then here I was, this fat ugly baby." She was putting it on a bit. But he liked it. She could tell it was making him happy, thinking what an ugly baby she'd been, and how much they'd wanted him.

18

THE PLACE WHERE Jason had disappeared was around the corner from the house. Connie had shown me a folder with all the newspaper stories. There was a picture of the drugstore where it happened and another of the baby-sitter and one of me. The baby-sitter's name was Debbie Klinger. She'd been seventeen years old. The newspaper said she was "distraught."

I went to the drugstore, and bought an ice cream cone, the way the baby-sitter had. She'd left me outside, in the stroller, where she could see me through the window. The weather had been good. She'd told the reporter if it had been raining, she would have taken me in the store with her.

She said it just took her a few minutes to buy the ice cream, then she went out and I was gone. That's what she said, but there must have been something else, some distraction. Maybe a friend walked in. Maybe she was looking at lipsticks or makeup, while outside, the kidnapper gave the stroller a push and then another push. When the stroller started moving, I probably didn't even look up. I always loved rides, being pushed, going fast. I wouldn't have known anything was wrong until I looked up and saw a strange face.

ON SATURDAY, CONNIE and I went food shopping together. Miller was at her friend's house. The weather was bad, rain and then snow and then rain again. She didn't invite me exactly. I invited myself. "I'll help you carry stuff."

"The way you're limping? What are you, a Saint Bernard? You going to hold the groceries in your teeth? You've been around Graham too much."

I laughed. I liked her sense of humor.

"You want anything special?" she said.

"Tapioca."

"I never make that."

"I know how," I said. "I love it. You just have to buy the box and add some milk."

"If you can make it, you can have it."

In the market, she said, "What's the Tapioca Kid think of this?" She showed me a can of baked beans.

"Good. Get it."

On the way home I asked her if I'd always liked tapioca. It was a leading question that went nowhere. She didn't remember. "Well, what did I eat?"

"I gave my kids all that awful baby stuff that looks like white glue."

"Like what?"

"Oh, I don't know . . . that rice cereal, whatever it was you gobbled it up. Both you kids were good eaters."

Both you kids were good eaters.

We had just turned into the driveway. The windows were steamed up and the wipers clicked back and forth. A smell of oranges and parsley rose from the groceries in back. *Both you kids.* That meant Miller, that meant Jason. That meant Miller and me.

It was warm inside the car but I shivered. She didn't move. I waited. Her hands rested on top of the wheel. She seemed to be thinking about something. *Both you kids . . .*

Yes, say it again! *Both you kids . . .* Say more! Keep talking!

Her hands slid around the wheel. "Better go in," she said, and she got out and started taking the packages in.

After we unloaded the groceries, Connie put me to work cutting up vegetables. "We're going to make pasta primavera," she said.

"What?"

"Spaghetti and vegetables with a fancy name. Miller hates it, but it's just you and me tonight." She showed me how to peel garlic by pressing the flat of the knife hard on the bulb and breaking through the surface. The way I wanted to break through with her.

"My grandmother didn't use garlic much," I said.

"When did you know?"

"That I didn't belong to them?" She nodded. "I always knew that." I looked her in the eye and lied.

I didn't say that I really didn't know until I stepped into the post office that day. But in a way, it was no lie. Everything I knew at the post office, I'd always known, from the beginning, someplace inside me.

"I always knew," I said again. "I always knew I wasn't like them. Not my grandmother, not my uncle."

"And your mother?"

"You mean Sharon? She wasn't my mother. I don't even remember her."

Connie tasted the sauce. "Do you remember when it happened?"

"I remember some things," I said. "I was scared." I didn't like that she expected me to remember things. "I cried."

"Oh! You cried! Of course you cried." My mother stopped and looked at me. She stroked my arm. "You cried . . ."

The fumes from the onion and garlic were making my eyes smart. Had I really cried? Saying it, I felt it was true. I could feel the tears now.

"WHAT DO YOU REMEMBER about the house?" Connie said while we were eating.

"Here?" I said. "My room. I had toys."

"Yes?"

"And . . . a bear. I think it was a bear. I used to throw it. I used to like to throw it on the floor."

"Yes, you did! I'd pick it up and you'd throw it down again." She laughed.

"I threw something out the window once," I said. I definitely remembered something, but then the memory got mixed up with me hanging out the window on 28th Street and dropping things. Once it was my grandmother's slippers. She went after me with a stick.

"You threw your monkey out the window," Connie said. "You remember that! That's amazing. Binko. Do you remember Binko?"

We sat there for a long time talking. Then we cleaned up together. Miller came home, and we all went upstairs to the living room and Connie played the piano. I sat on the floor near her with a set of bongos between my knees. I watched her play, the way her fingers ran over the keyboard, bunched together one moment then all knuckles and joints the next. Her fingers were like dancers or acrobats, all jumping, then tumbling after each other. I caught the beat on the drums and followed along.

"You learn fast," Connie said.

Miller looked up from her book.

Connie showed me some stuff in a lesson book. "If you practice the things I've marked, you'll improve fast."

"I'll practice every day," I said. I could see she liked that. We sat together at the piano and she showed me how to finger the scale. I knew she liked me, and I said to myself, *Just be patient.*

19

"YOU'RE LIMPING WORSE than before," Connie said to me a few days later. "Let me see that foot. Put it up on the chair."

"I'm okay," I said, but when she touched my ankle I winced.

"I bet you broke something, after all. That looks ugly. I'm taking you to the emergency room."

In the hospital, we waited an hour before we saw Dr. Greenkey, the orthopedic surgeon. "What have you been doing with this foot, driving nails with it? How did this happen?"

"I tripped over my own feet."

"About a week and a half ago," Connie said.

The doctor nodded. She was wearing shorts and a T-shirt with whales. "I'm going to send you for X rays. As soon as they're developed, I'll talk to you again."

The X rays showed nothing broken. "That's good," I said. "Right, Mom?"

"A sprain can be worse than a break," Dr. Greenkey said.

"It's a soft tissue tear. If you don't take care of it, healing can be protracted." She put my foot in an air cast. "Your son should really be on crutches," she told Connie.

I glanced at my mother. She nodded.

"Make sure he keeps his foot elevated as much as possible. Keep the weight off it. You don't want to have to go into surgery."

Connie found a pair of crutches for me in the attic. She'd used them years ago after a ski accident. They fit me perfectly.

For a while, I really stayed off my foot. I sat around in the living room watching TV with my foot up on a stool or I'd lie on the floor and prop my foot against the wall.

Look at me, Mom. I'm resting. I'm keeping my foot elevated the way I'm supposed to. I'm letting it heal. I'm being good! I've been good all along, haven't I? Almost two weeks of being good good good. So how about it? Stop being so stingy! You know I'm Jason. You looked the doctor in the eye when she called me your son. You know I'm your son! Why don't you admit it? Give a little. How long is it going to take you people to figure this out?

I WAS IN MY ROOM when I heard Miller say, "That's him." She and another girl looked in, then whizzed by. I was on the bed. Every time they went by my room I looked up and said, "Hi."

Finally, her friend sort of leaned into the room. She was tall, with bangs and hair down to her shoulders. "I'm Francesca. How's your foot?"

"Still there. It's great. No, I'm lying. It's really hurting."

"Come on, Francesca," Miller said. "We've got things to do."

"Wait a sec." Francesca leaned in farther. "So you're Miller's brother. I'm glad I'm meeting you."

"Me, too. You're cute. I like all my sister's friends."

"How many have you met?"

"You're the only one so far. What did my sister tell you about me? Whatever she said, it's all true."

"Francesca!" Miller pulled her away. "We've got things to do. Come on."

"Miller, stop! I think it's fantastic that you're back," Francesca continued. "I think it's the most exciting thing that's ever happened around here."

"Most exciting thing," Miller mimicked.

"Shut up!" Francesca said, "I'm having an interesting conversation with Jason. Was it hard coming back, Jason? Where were you? Where did you live? Did they keep you locked up a lot? Did you have to run away?"

"Does he look like they kept him locked up?" Miller said.

I really liked hearing her call me Jason. I wanted her to go on talking to me, saying my name, but Miller dragged her away. It cheered me up though. Francesca didn't stumble over my name. It came out nice and smooth, like she'd been saying it and hearing it a lot. Miller hadn't called me Jason since she introduced me to her stepmother in the country club that first day. But she must have been talking about Jason to her friend.

20

BRUCE CAUGHT ME watching TV in the staff room and said, "Why are you hanging around? Do something useful. Wash the car."

"Okay." I got the cleaning supplies and connected the hose to the outside faucet. I limped around on one crutch and blasted the car with water. I didn't mind washing the car, but I couldn't stand my father's attitude. He either treated me like a servant or acted like I didn't exist.

Why are you hanging around? What did he think I was doing here? What were any of them thinking about? All I wanted was for one of them to say, *He's here! God almighty, it's Jason!* Just once. Just once act like something real had happened. Why was it so hard for them to say it?

They were a bunch of sleepwalkers. The whole family was asleep! When were they going to wake up? The Eddie in me was impatient. He was pissed off. He'd had enough! *Walk out on these guys! They had their chance. You don't get a second chance. Say good-bye, say you'll be seeing them someday—maybe. You'll send them a postcard with no return address. That'll give them something to think about.*

When I got through with the outside of the car I sat inside and polished the dashboard. I let the window down and put my arm out. Maybe I'd drive by Miller's school and park in front, maybe drive one wheel up on the sidewalk.

When I was finished, I called my father out and showed him the car. "Nice," he said. "Very nice job." He gave me a pat on the back, and I began to feel really good. His hand on my shoulder . . . Then he took out money and tried to give it to me. He insulted me. It wasn't money I wanted from him. Maybe Eddie was ready for a handout, but Jason washed the car for his father because he felt like it, because it was his father's car and, therefore, his car, and he liked doing things for his father.

I pushed the money away. "No charge. Any time you want it washed, you just say so."

"I owe you one. When are you coming in for your teeth?"

My teeth! He didn't get it. Jason was standing there—his son! *Here I am. You've had plenty of time to look at me. Do you like the way your son turned out? Do you like me? Do you hate me? What do you think? Do you want me? Give me an answer!*

Maybe Jason could be patient. He kept saying his family would come around in time, but Eddie was sick of waiting. He wasn't used to waiting, to being nice, to being patient. Those who waited got nothing! You had to get into people's faces and say, *What are you going to do about it!* Jason wanted an answer, too. He wasn't really so calm. He wanted somebody to acknowledge him. If his father wasn't going to do it, if his mother couldn't make up her mind, that left his baby sister. All she had to say was, *There's my brother! There's Jason!*

21

SOMETHING WOKE MILLER. She thought it was Graham prowling. She turned and covered her head with the blanket. She was sunk down in the tangle and muss of sleep. "Miller." She opened one eye. He was standing by her bed, leaning on his crutch.

She sat up. "What time is it?"

"Time to get up. Come on. Let's go. I'll wait for you downstairs."

She looked at the clock. It was one in the morning. "What're you doing?"

"I'm going out. You want to go with me or not?"

A nervous energy shot out of him and infected her. She said, "Wait for me downstairs." She dressed quickly, grabbed her jacket, then went silently down the stairs. Graham tried to follow her, but she pushed him back inside. Wait till she told Francesca about this.

It was spooky to be out this late, but exciting, too. They set off down the street. It was dark, a scattering of lights, a few cars on the road, streetlights hidden in the shadowy trees. She could almost see her parents' worried faces hovering in the shadows. Worried, cautious, afraid for her every minute. *Where are you going? How long are you going to stay out? Who are you going with? Come straight home afterward.* This was the first year her mother hadn't insisted on having somebody in the house when she left on a weekend gig.

All that worry was in Miller's blood. She'd breathed it in with every breath she took. She wanted to worry less and do more. *That's* why she'd come out with her brother tonight. He wasn't afraid of the dark, he didn't worry every minute. She'd always known that about him, even before he came home.

He was wearing one of her father's big hats. There were certain views of him that were just like her father. Glancing at his profile, at the stillness in his face, she was drawn to him. She even liked the way he used the crutches. A step, then he'd swing on the crutches, then another step. Sometimes, like a rabbit, he took a great leap and came down on his good foot, catching himself with the crutches. Once he dropped his hat and scooped it up with the end of the crutch.

"Where'd you get the hat?" she said.

"Dad gave it to me. I went out to the ranch the other day. I hitched a ride with some Boy Scouts."

"Wow." She had more questions, but she didn't feel the need to ask him every little thing the way her parents did. Of course, they were always trying to figure out if he was really Jason. She didn't know either. She wanted him to be her brother, and maybe that was enough.

This was exactly what she'd imagined so many times—her brother home and the two of them off on an adventure together. She felt as if the whole town belonged to them. Everyone else was asleep in their warm beds. She felt bold and dangerous, ready for anything.

Crossing the Hunt's Road bridge, there was a steady stream of traffic. The plastic factory on the other side of the river must have been changing shifts. They leaned over the railing and looked down at the river far below them. "I never look down from this height without imagining climbing over the guardrail," she said.

"Yeah, it would be so easy."

He was looking straight down at the water. It wasn't Jason that she saw now. It wasn't Eddie, either. It was a stranger with a face emptied of all feeling. In that instant she could imagine him throwing her off the bridge. She stepped back and walked away.

He caught up with her and they continued down streets of dark shuttered stores and little houses. This was a part of town she didn't know. None of her friends lived here. Suddenly he said, "Why don't you ever call me Jason?"

"I do."

"No you don't. You did it one time. Call me Jason."

"I will when I feel like it." She hated being ordered around.

He stopped in front of Bruno's 24 Hour Comfort Motel and Restaurant. A pink sign shed a garish light across the sidewalk.

"Let's go," she said.

"Wait. I want something to eat."

"In there?" She followed him reluctantly.

The lobby was empty and nobody was behind the reception desk. In a dark room a few people sat drinking at a bar. They sat down at a table. Miller looked around uneasily. There was nobody here even remotely her age, but the waiter turned out to be a boy she recognized from school. He had a sister named Gloria that she talked to sometimes.

"I'll have a cheese sandwich and a cherry soda," Jason said. She ordered a diet soda, and kept her head down.

When the food came, Jason pushed half his sandwich toward her. She took a bite and passed it back. He carefully spread mustard between the slices of bread. He was deft, like her father. Her mother, too. They were both people who did things with their hands. She looked at her own stumpy square hands. She didn't even have nice handwriting.

When the check came, Jason handed it to her with a smile. He looked really pleased as he gave her the empty hand, empty pocket gesture. No money. Super! It was his idea to come in here. What if she didn't have money either? What then, call Mom and Dad? She could just imagine that. Her mother would be so mad she wouldn't sleep the rest of the night. Her father would come for her. He might leave Jason here, though, to wash dishes. Lucky Jason that she happened to have enough money. She paid, but she was mad. He expected everything to be handed to him, like he was a prince or something.

She would have left him right then, but she didn't want to walk home alone. What had she even come out for? She had school tomorrow—he didn't. He had no routine, no schedule. There was nothing he had to do, except wake her up in the middle of the night and invite her out to watch him eat.

"Let's go," she said.

He wasn't in any rush. He went across the corridor to a game room and started playing a road game.

"Where'd you get the money?" she said.

He shrugged and didn't look up. He'd had money all along. She was so mad at him she walked away. He came after her and opened the patio doors to the indoor pool. He lay down at the edge of the pool and tried to float one of his crutches, then he tried to touch the underwater lights. He was like a little kid.

"Do you want to go swimming?" he said.

"I didn't remember to bring my bathing suit."

He just laughed. "I don't even own one, sister. If I go in, will you?"

She really hated him. Now he was mocking her, saying things that he knew would embarrass her.

They went back to the game room and played Ping-Pong. She wasn't going to play with him at first. He couldn't play on crutches, but he tossed them aside. "I'm a good player," he said.

He wasn't. He held the paddle wrong. She kept piling up the points. He tossed the paddle down in disgust at the end of every game, then picked it up and challenged her to one more game. And lost again. She could have let him win, but she didn't feel like it. She beat him eighteen games in a row.

She was poised for his serve when he said, "Why don't you ever call me Jason?" He had the paddle in one hand and the ball in the other. "Don't you believe me, or do you all think the same thing?"

Did she believe him? If she did, why didn't she just say so? And if she didn't, why be so careful with him? Why not just say what she thought?

"Don't you see that I wouldn't be here if I didn't belong here?" He dropped his paddle and came around the table toward her. "My little sister," he said. "My baby sister. Why don't you love me?" He grabbed her arm.

He was hurting her. "Stop that! I don't like you when you're this way. I don't like to be mauled."

"Mauled?" he repeated. "What's that, something you do

in a mall? Or do you mail it? You're so smart, so many big words. So much smarter than me."

She was close to tears. "I thought you were a nice person. Why are you doing this?"

"I'm not nice. Why should I be nice? Nobody's ever been nice to me."

She knew he meant his past, where he'd lived before with his crazy grandmother and uncle, but he meant her and Mom and Dad, too. Suddenly, it struck her that her mother had done this incredibly naive thing of taking a complete stranger into their house, and now she had done an even more naive thing by going off with him in the middle of the night, and then making it worse by coming to this sleazy motel. There was nobody around. They were alone in the game room.

"There must have been some good things in your life," she said. She was trying to calm him down while she figured out what to do next.

"Good things happen to people like you. Just bad things happen to people like me."

She couldn't bear his self-pity. She wanted to walk out, but he was still holding her. If he knew how much she despised him right now . . .

"I bet you think it's bad to lie and cheat and steal," he said. "*Nice* people don't do those things. Oh, no. Nothing's bad if it saves you from being hit, but you don't know what being hit means. You know what's bad? Being hit in the face is bad. Have you ever been punched in the face?"

"Let me go!"

He twisted her arm behind her. "This is what my uncle Stew used to do to me for fun. He'd twist my arm till I screamed."

"I'm Miller Diaz, I'm not your stupid uncle!"

"And I'm Jason Diaz. Admit it, say I'm your brother."

"You don't act like a brother."

"How's a brother supposed to act? I don't know. Tell me."

"Not like this!"

He let her go and she walked out. She almost ran. She thought of calling her parents, but she didn't want to stay in this place another second. On the street, she walked fast, keeping to the side of the road. She rubbed her arm. Oh, she was glad she hadn't cried. She would never let him see her cry! She never wanted to be near him again.

How could she have been so blind? Her brother? He wasn't her brother. Just because he was good-looking and had a nice face didn't make him Jason. There was so much anger in him. She wasn't used to being around people like that. She got angry, and so did her mother and her father, and even nice nice Mary Anne. Everyone got angry. But Jason—or Eddie—or whoever he was was angry in a different way. He covered it up with smiles and being nice and helping out. And all the time there was that fire in him.

Ahead of her, a traffic light turned amber, then red. Cars slowed. If he came after her, she would jump into any car. She looked back. He was on the other side of the street, stepping, hopping, trying to catch up to her.

She stepped into the road, but then the light changed and all the cars sped away. "Get away from me," she yelled.

"I know I didn't act nice. Are you going to tell them?"

"I'll do whatever I feel like doing." She ran across the street.

"Wait up! I can't walk!"

"Tough," she muttered and kept going.

22

CRAZY EDDIE. Jason would have had more sense. I went over to Miller's school to talk to her, but a teacher, or maybe it was the principal, stopped me at the door. "Who are you?" He had a tie squeezed tight around his fat neck.

"Jason Diaz." I gave him a smile. I hated guys like him—they thought they ran the world.

"You don't go to this school." It wasn't a question.

"No."

"Where do you go?"

"I don't live around here."

"What's your business?"

"I want to see my sister."

"Is it an emergency?"

"No."

"If it isn't an emergency you can wait until after school."

"I just want to talk to her for a minute."

"You can't just walk in here any time you want to."

"I'm Jason Diaz."

"I don't care if you're King Tut. Get out."

I went outside and sat down on the steps. If he came out and said anything to me, I'd tell him it was a free country and I could sit anywhere I wanted.

A girl went by. She was tall, wearing dark pants and a pink sweater. "What happened to your foot, cutie?"

"I tripped."

"Tripped over your laces," she mocked. "Does it hurt?"

"I'm brave."

"You only cry to your mommy, I know. Can I try out your crutches?" She took them and hopped off. When she brought them back, she said, "I'm Naomi. What's your name?"

"Jason Diaz. I'm waiting for my sister."

Naomi's eyes opened large. "Miller Diaz is your sister? I don't believe it. You're too cute to be her brother. Do you feel superior, too, because your father's a dentist?"

"It's nice to be rich," I said.

Naomi gave me a mean smile. "Oh, you are Miller's brother, aren't you?" She started to walk away.

"Hey, Naomi."

"What?"

"It was a pleasure talking to you."

When Miller finally came out of school the buses were loading. "Miller!" She saw me, but she kept going. "I have to talk to you," I said, following her.

"I don't want to talk to you."

"I'm sorry about last night." Kids kept moving around us, getting on the bus. I had the feeling I was being looked over. *Look all you want. It's me, Jason Diaz talking to his sister, Miller Diaz.* "I didn't mean to scare you."

"Don't flatter yourself. I'm not scared, I'm mad."

"You should be mad."

"Shut up! Don't tell me what I should be. Don't tell me what I shouldn't be. Don't tell me anything!"

"Do you hate me?" I leaned on the crutches. "Everybody else does."

"What are you talking about?"

"I'm talking about me. Jason. I'm here, but I might as well be in China. If I left now, you wouldn't even care. You wouldn't even say good-bye to me."

"What's your idea of good-bye—strangling someone?"

"On or off?" the bus driver called. Miller got on and the bus doors closed.

"Listen, can't we talk about it?" I called as the bus drove off.

MILLER WENT PAST my room. "Hey, sis," I said. She went by without a word. "Sis!" I called after her. "Talk to me."

The door to her room slammed.

I knocked on her door, then went in. She was sitting on the floor with Graham.

"Don't you know what a closed door means?"

"Why are you still mad at me?"

"I don't know what you're talking about. And I'm not your sis. And while I'm at it, tell your ignorant friends not to talk to me."

"What friends? You mean Naomi?" I sat down on the floor next to her.

"Yes, Naomi Ridley and that idiot friend of hers with the blond streaks in his hair, Flash Herron."

"Who?"

"He doesn't have the brain of an ant. He talked to me today. I never talk to him. I've never said a word to him and believe me I don't miss it."

We sat there. I kept glancing at her. Every time she scowled, I wanted to laugh. She was cute. I'd liked her from the minute I saw her. "So, how come you don't take my apology?" I said. "You know the other night wasn't me. That wasn't Jason."

"I know it wasn't Jason!"

"Something came over me. I just got in a mood. Eddie gets into rotten moods. I'm Jason, but sometimes I act like Eddie. I was Eddie for so long, I can't help it."

"Oh, please!" She snorted. "Don't give me that. Like you're not responsible for yourself!"

"I once got so mad at my grandmother I pulled everything out of the refrigerator and smashed it on the floor."

"Eggs?"

"Yeah, the eggs. Milk. I stepped on the tomatoes. I poured pancake syrup over everything."

"What'd your grandmother do?"

"She threw me out the window."

"She threw you out the window? I never heard of anything like that. How high up were you?"

"Four stories."

"I don't believe it."

"Yeah, she did. I was a mess."

Her face crumpled. "That's horrible!"

I nodded.

"What are you smiling about?" she said. "Is that a story? Did you just make that up?"

"Not all of it," I said. "It's mostly true."

"I don't know what to believe with you, Jason Eddie. You've got a story for everything, don't you?"

"Bruce told you I make up stories, didn't he?"

"I don't know what you're talking about." She combed through Graham's hair.

I counted the pictures on the wall. I counted the china horses she collected. "Tell Miller to talk to me," I said to Graham. "A sister should talk to her brother, and if he does something dumb, she ought to hit him and forget it."

"Tell my so-called brother," she said to Graham, "that I don't inflict violence on people."

"You mean hit?" I said.

"And who says I'm your sister?"

"You wouldn't care what I did, if you weren't my sister."

"You're right in my face! I don't have any choice. You think I want to think about you all the time? My brother wouldn't act the way you did. My brother wouldn't talk to Naomi Ridley. He'd laugh in her dumb face."

I worked my fingers around my sore ankle. "Miller. How do you know you're really you?"

She looked at me. "What's that supposed to mean?"

"How do you know you're really Miller?"

"I know because I'm not making it up," she said.

"They told you that you were theirs, but what if they were lying to you? What if they picked you up somewhere or bought you or stole you the way I was stolen?"

She got a brush and started really brushing Graham hard. "I wish you wouldn't say things like that," she said finally.

"Why?"

"Because I can't stay mad at you when you say it."

"Hey! That's great." I reached over and sort of patted her shoulder.

"Don't!" She pushed my hand away. "What were you and Naomi Ridley talking about?"

"Naomi and me? Nothing."

"Come on! You know. You were talking to her that day at school. I saw you give her your crutches."

"You saw that?"

"Yes, I saw it. I was looking out the window."

"Why didn't you let me know you were there? What'd you think I was there for? I was waiting for you, remember?"

"I didn't want to talk to you. Remember?"

"She thinks I'm cute," I said.

"Who does?"

"Your friend, Naomi."

"I told you she's no friend of mine. She drinks, and I don't mean from a baby bottle. I can't believe you find somebody like her interesting. What did you tell her?"

"I told her you were my sister."

"What else?"

"And I was your brother."

"And what else?"

"She wanted to know if I was as big a snob as you are. I said it was nice to be rich."

"Did you really say that?" Miller snorted, then put her face next to Graham's. "He has the nerve for anything, doesn't he, Graham?"

23

"I WANT TO TALK TO YOU," Connie said, walking into my room.

"Sure, Mom." I flipped off the stereo.

She took a cigarette out of her pocket. "Not here. In the living room." She walked out and sat at the piano with the cigarette in her mouth.

"I thought you didn't smoke anymore, Mom."

"I'm not smoking. I just like the feeling of it in my mouth."

I sat down on the couch. "Let me have one, then." She handed me a cigarette. Cool, I thought, me and my mom, both of us sitting here with unlit cigarettes. "Look at us, Mom." I laughed.

"Are you Jason?" she said.

"What?"

"I thought I would know," she said. "You look like him. You look the way he would have looked. At least . . . I think so. I might not know if you passed me on the street, but you've been in this house for two weeks, and I should know for sure, by now. There should be something about you that tells me with absolute certainty."

"This." I touched the scar over my eyebrow.

"I don't mean that sort of thing. That's something, but it's not enough. I'm talking about *knowing,* knowing inside, a sixth sense, knowing the way any mother knows her child."

"You knew," I said. "You knew, didn't you? Remember when you first saw me?"

She struck a couple of keys. "The longer you stay here, the more I wonder, and the more I wonder, the more uncertain I am. I can't live this way. It's making me frantic. I'm not sleeping . . . I can't enjoy anything . . ."

"Hey, Mom, I'm sorry . . ."

"You don't know anything about Jason, do you?"

"I do. I know things."

"What do you know?" She hit a chord. "Do you know me? Tell me you know me. Did you know *me* when you saw me the first night? Did you know I was your mother?"

I met her eyes. I put the cigarette aside and pulled myself up. *Let there be no doubt.* "I'm Jason," I said. "I am Jason." I was quiet. Maybe I was too quiet. Maybe I should have raised my voice a little, maybe yelled.

"Come here." She pulled me down next to her on the piano bench and put her arms around me. It didn't feel natural to be held that way. My neck started to hurt. When my grandmother had held me, it was to stop me from doing something, and when I got too big for her, she threw things at me.

I didn't move. My mother was waiting for something to happen. I was waiting too. We both waited. Waited for something past words to tell us that I was Jason, the child she had lost.

My mother released me and took some papers from the top of the piano. "We've got a problem," she said.

A problem could be anything. Maybe she needed money. Did we need to tighten our belts? I'd go to work if she wanted me to.

"The first thing is the address you gave us. Rugby Road."

"Rugby Road?" My stomach didn't feel that great.

"You look surprised. Rugby Road. You gave us a number. You described a house—white with a green roof and there was a garden. It sounded so pretty. Bruce had a man check it out."

"A man?"

"An investigator. He checked out the story you gave us. He couldn't find the house or Lorraine Leonard, either, not on Rugby Road. There was a Lorraine Leonard on Twenty-eighth Street, but that's a long way from Rugby Road. No single-family houses on Twenty-eighth Street, just apartments and a potato chip plant."

I got up. My foot was like a weight dragging after me. What did they need an investigator for? Didn't they have their own eyes? I was Jason. "I told you. I keep telling you . . . I'm Jason. I belong here. I'm Jason."

She pointed at me with her unlit cigarette. "You're a poor boy. You've had a hard life, you don't know your father, you don't remember your mother. I know you want to be Jason, but when I ask you anything, all you know is Eddie Leonard. You lived on Twenty-eighth Street, didn't you?"

"Yes."

"You lived there with your grandmother."

"Yes. Until she died."

"Rugby Road was a story."

"Yes."

"The landlord—"

"Anton." I leaned on the crutches. "He doesn't know anything. What did he say?"

"He said he never saw your grandmother leave the house. He said she was on welfare and she sent you out for everything she needed."

"She did leave the house. She went to work." I banged the crutches on the floor. Rugby Road was a lie, but this was a *real* lie. "My grandmother worked. She worked all the time. She was a bookkeeper, until she had a heart attack."

"Okay, I'm sorry."

"Me, too. I just started saying that thing about Rugby Road, and I couldn't stop. I didn't want you to know about Twenty-eighth Street. It's not that nice. It's not Walcott Street. I told you a story, but it was only because I didn't want to come to you like a beggar. Anyway, what difference does it make where I lived?"

"The difference is that you didn't tell us the truth. Why didn't you say this in the first place? I don't understand."

Didn't she really? Didn't she ever exaggerate? Didn't she ever make things up? Sometimes you had to make up stories. You did it to make things nicer. It wasn't like stealing or killing someone.

"Do you really think it would have made any difference to us where you lived?" she said. "You're a child, you don't choose your home. We wouldn't judge you by where you lived. What else did you tell us that wasn't true? What about you and school?"

"I did all right in school."

"But not as wonderfully as you tried to make us believe."

"I'm Jason."

"Are you?"

"I am." I stood there, my hands clasped together like I was praying. Or was I handcuffed? All I'd ever wanted was for them to accept me, to give me a chance, to trust me, but they'd never trusted me. They'd acted so nice, but all the time they'd been investigating me. It had been pretend from the beginning. I threw my crutches aside. "I'm not the liar here!" I shouted.

Connie rubbed out the cigarette. "I can't live this way. I want you to go. Live somewhere else. I don't believe you . . . or maybe I do, but you still have to go."

I studied my mother's face. She could be just trying to scare me. It could be the stereo. "Did Miller say anything about her stereo, Mom? If she wants it, I'll give it back."

"What are you talking about? Didn't you hear what I said?"

"Okay." I smiled, I acted like I didn't care, but I was scared. I was dizzy, and part of me seemed far away already. I thought of my grandmother's apartment and Twenty-eighth Street. Where was I supposed to go? This was home. There was no other place. "I'm Jas—"

"Stop! I don't want to hear it. You don't know you're Jason any more than I do. And stop looking at me like that! Why do you always give me those pleading eyes?" She tried to pull a cigarette from the pack, and broke it. "Damn!"

"Mom—"

"I'm not your mom."

"Who is, if you aren't?"

"Jesus! What are you doing to me? Level with me for once."

"I do."

"I want the truth."

"I tell you the truth."

Her eyes, her hands, went from one thing to another. "Who are you? Tell me. Who are you? Who are you really?"

"Hey . . ." I smiled at her. I was trying to be relaxed. "Like I keep telling you, Mom, I'm Jason."

"Don't be cute with me. Don't you have any other answer? Are you a broken record? Is your needle stuck?"

She ran and turned up all the lights in the room, then came back and held me and looked into my eyes. Her fingers bit into my shoulders. "You don't know if you're my son. How can you know? You were a baby. How can you know, if I don't know?" Suddenly she pulled me toward her and sniffed me all around my head, then pushed me away again.

"Mom, I've been practicing the music you showed me." I sat down at the piano. "I've got those scales down cold." I played them for her, first with the right hand, then with the left hand, then with both hands. "See?" I turned but she was gone.

I found her in my room, emptying the drawers. "Get your knapsack," she said. "Take everything. Don't leave anything behind."

"Mom!"

"Call me Mom again, I'm going to scream." She threw my things into the pack. "Go! Don't talk. Let's go!" She herded me down the stairs. "We're going to keep in touch. I don't want you to take this personally. I just need some distance. You can get a room at the Y. I'm not abandoning you. I'll pay your rent, I'll give you money for food, and I want you to register for school."

Bruce came out in the hall. "What's going on?" He was wearing his white coat. "It sounded like you were tearing the house apart."

I sat down on the stairs. I couldn't look at Bruce. I felt ashamed. "Mom's putting me out."

"Connie?" Bruce said.

"I want him to go to the Y. He can live there as well as here."

"What happened?"

"You know damn well what happened! The report. You were right, I was too quick to take him in."

"What'd you expect, Connie, an untouched angel? Did you think you were going to get a perfect son back?"

"Hey! Who are you to talk? You're the one who kept talking about facts."

"Right. But I didn't talk about a perfect son."

"I don't want to have this discussion now, Bruce. Don't you get righteous on me. I'm feeling horrible! I could be putting my own son out of the house."

"Leave him to me," Bruce said.

"You?"

"I'll take care of him."

She hesitated. "Good," she said, then went back upstairs.

He stood there, studying me.

Don't move I told myself. Don't say anything. They want you out of their house, okay, you don't want their charity.

24

MILLER AND JASON were dancing around the room. Her brother was home. Everybody was happy. Their whole family was together. The music throbbed through the walls. Then she woke up.

She couldn't get the dream out of her mind. She told her mother, "I had a wonderful dream."

Her mother had her trumpet apart on the table. She was cleaning it.

"We've got to bring Eddie home." It was so obvious. Her mother didn't have to be sad about Jason anymore. All she had to do was let Eddie fill that place in her heart.

Her mother put down the mouthpiece. "What was your dream?"

"That was it. I mean, Eddie and I were dancing—but when I woke up, I knew it meant he should come home."

Her mother ran a cloth across the bright metal.

"Mom, you didn't have to put him out."

"We talked about this already."

"All right, so he told a few little fibs. He's not perfect, but like you always say, who is?"

"Miller, it's not about perfection. It's about uncertainty. It's seeing him every day and wondering, is he really Jason?"

"Why can't he just be who he is? Does it matter that much if he's really Jason or not?"

"Yes."

"I don't get it. I can't even think about Jason anymore without imagining Eddie first."

"Exactly. He's almost become Jason. And what if he isn't? What if our Jason walks in tomorrow or next week or next year?"

"Mom! So we'll love him, too." Then she thought of something else. "What if Jason never comes home, Mom?"

Her mother put the trumpet back in its case and closed the lid. "If I knew what had become of him, I think I could let go."

Miller knew it was useless to go on arguing, but she couldn't stop. "Eddie might even be a better son than Jason because he would always know we chose him."

"Miller—"

"We've got room. He needs us."

"That's not reason enough."

"You need him. And you love him. I know you do."

Her mother sat there with her hands on the closed instrument case. "I know, that's what makes it so hard."

25 THE NIGHT CONNIE threw me out Bruce drove me out to the ranch. He said I could sleep in the barn. "Cool," I said. I would have slept anywhere. I was ready to sleep on the floor in the living room, but if Bruce wanted me in the barn that was okay, too.

"Hey!" I said. "Hey!" I tapped him on the arm a few times. I was trying to feel good. "Hey! Hey! You're really getting to like me, aren't you?"

"Yeah, you're a good kid. That's not the problem."

"I know I take some getting used to. And I understand about Connie. It's not easy to see that I'm Jason, because I was just three the last time you guys saw me."

"You've got the idea," he said. In the barn he threw a tarp over some bales of hay, then gave me a sheet and a couple of blankets. "How's that?"

"It's good. Thanks."

Bruce picked up some leather harnesses from the ground and hung them on the wall. "You're right, it's been a long time."

"I know! A long time! Maybe you didn't recognize me. That's okay. I understand!"

He stared at me. "It's true you . . . Jason could have changed so much I wouldn't recognize him."

"I'm Jason. Jason Diaz."

"Listen, I know what it's like to be poor. I know about heating with the gas stove and being on welfare. My parents came here from Puerto Rico. Are you listening? My parents worked hard, and I worked hard. I worked for everything I have. Do you understand what I'm saying? Poor doesn't matter. Are you my son—that's what matters."

"Sure," I said.

"Sure? Is that it? Look, I'm not going to be mad. If it's a story, it's a story. That's okay. Who sent you? Do you know something you haven't said? Do you know about Jason? Did you hear something from somebody? I want to know what happened to him. Is it over with, is it finished? If you know something, Eddie, for God's sake tell me, so I can close the file and lock it and know my son is at rest."

"Dad . . ."

He looked at me.

"Dad."

He shook his head and walked out.

I WOKE IN THE middle of the night. The horses banged in their wooden stalls. My thoughts raced. I had been here three nights and three days. Would Connie ever let me back in the house? I missed Miller.

I got up and went out. It was a dark clouded night. I went across the field, and into the house. I let myself in quietly and used the phone downstairs. I dialed my grandmother's number. I'd left the phone on the floor near the TV, and I imagined my grandmother answering it. I could see her getting out of bed, grumbling, and yelling for me. "Eddie, you little bastard, answer the phone!" I let it ring about ten times and then I hung up and went out.

The dogs followed me to the road. The crutches dug into my armpits. I walked along the side of the road. A white fog sat in the hollows. I zipped up my jacket and buttoned my collar. Sometimes a car passed. Headlights threw my shadow ahead of me, a long shape between two sticks. I remembered a wooden toy I once had. Squeeze the sticks and the wooden boy in the middle jumped and did tricks. Like me, doing my tricks for Bruce and Connie, trying so hard to belong, to please.

Sometimes a car slowed down. Two scenarios ran in my head like two channels, each one with a different story. In one scenario, a car tried to run me off the road. In the other story, a car stopped, Miller was in it, and we drove home together.

I swung on my crutches. Swing. Step. One swing I was Jason, the next I was Eddie. A van honked as it passed. "Wah hoooo!" I yelled. My voice bounced off the mountain. "Wah . . . hoooo!"

The van pulled up ahead. "You want a ride, man?" someone called.

"Why not?" The van was full of kids. I climbed in the back, and lay the crutches on the floor. "Where you going, man?"

"The same place you're going."

"You're Jason, aren't you?" a girl said.

It was Naomi, the girl who'd borrowed my crutches. Someone passed me a can of beer. "See," Naomi said to the driver, "I told you I knew him, Flash. We're friends."

"Who isn't your friend, Naomi?" Flash had two blond streaks in his hair.

Naomi traded places with another girl and sat next to me.

"Pass the beverage," Flash said. He took a swallow, then banged the horn. He spit in the can. "Who wants a drink? Naomi? Want an after-dinner cocktail?"

"Disgusting!"

"What's wrong with spit? I didn't pee in it."

"Pig."

"Oink oink!" Flash said. "How about your new boyfriend? Where you from, man?"

"Big city."

"Why'd you come to this boring place?"

"I came to see my family."

"He's a native," Naomi said. "His father is Dr. Diaz, the dentist. His sister is Miller Diaz."

Flash turned. "I know her. Little chubby girl? You her brother? How come I never saw you before? I thought I knew everybody in this dump."

"I've been away," I said.

"Away?"

"Yeah. A long time."

"Hey! Are you the one who disappeared? I know that story. Your father's got a ranch, right? My father sold him his tractor. My father said there was something fishy about the way you disappeared. He said nobody disappears without a trace. So where have you been?"

"Is that true?" Naomi said. "You disappeared? I didn't know that."

"Is this the fastest this junk can go?" I said.

"Junk! This is my mom's brand new van, man. It hasn't even got twelve hundred miles on it." The van spurted forward. "Going for eighty . . . ninety . . . is that fast enough for you?" The car swerved from side to side. "Want a hundred?"

The Eddie part of me laughed. Jason knew the driver was an idiot. Eddie put his arm around Naomi and kissed her.

The horn blared at a car coming the other way. "Hey, Jason," Flash said. "You ever do this in the big city? You ever drive with your eyes shut?" He turned around with his back to the road. "Count. One . . . two . . ."

The van sped down the dark road, swinging from side to side.

"Cut it out, Flash, you're making me seasick," a guy behind me said.

". . . eight . . . nine. I'm going for fifteen and the world championship."

"Flash, you idiot. There's a car coming!"

"Damn it! You're going to hit—" I grabbed the wheel. The van swerved across the road and back, then slammed into a guardrail. I was flung into the front seat.

Flash was groaning. "My mother's car." The doors were jammed shut. We climbed out the windows.

Flash tried to lift the van off the rail. "She's going to kill me," he cried.

I sat down on the railing. Somebody handed me the crutches just as the cops appeared. One car, then another coming from the other direction, red lights flashing.

26

THE POLICE PUT ME in a narrow room by myself. They took the crutches away. There was a table in the room. I sat on the table, my back against the wall. No window. The sort of room they put you in to make you think. I closed my eyes and I was back on 28th Street . . . locked in, lying on the floor, kicking the door. I could hear my grandmother running the water in the other room. The TV was on. *Let me out. I'll be good. I promise.*

I opened my eyes. The walls were a no-color gray, but they seemed to have a red tint. The red room had been this small, only it had been good. I had felt safe there, protected.

I reached out with my good foot and pushed the door. "Hey," I yelled. "Someone!" When were they going to let me out? Maybe when they found out I didn't have a family that wanted me, they'd put me away somewhere.

A policewoman questioned me. Her name tag said Corporal Denise Taggert.

"Name?" she asked.

I shook my head.

"No name? Really? How old are you?"

I hesitated. If I said I was fifteen, they'd put me into a home. "Seventeen. I'm going to be eighteen next month."

"Address?"

"No address."

"No address?"

"No permanent address. I'm in transition."

"Now, come on, your parents aren't going to be that mad at you. We have to call them to come get you."

There was picture on the desk of her son. Was he home now? When she came home did he call her Mommy or Corporal Denise?

"How did the accident happen?"

"I don't know."

"Who was driving?"

"I don't know. I was walking, and they picked me up."

"They're your friends?"

"No, I don't really know them."

"What's your father's name? What's your phone number?"

"Why do you want to call him?"

"That's our procedure here. We don't just let you go."

"He isn't going to care. He won't come here."

"Why don't you give him a chance? I'm sure he cares."

I shook my head.

She got up and stepped away from the desk.

I looked around. I could walk out. Once I was outside, I'd pick up a ride. Wherever the car went, that's where I'd go.

Corporal Taggert came back with my crutches. "Okay, Jason. I don't know why you made things so hard for yourself. I just called your father and he's coming right down."

"How'd you know my name?"

"Your friends told me."

"My father's coming?"

"He's not going to kill you. If this is the only stupid thing you do in your life, you'll be okay. Why don't you go clean up now?"

In the bathroom, I brushed dirt off my pants. I didn't bother tucking my shirt in.

I saw myself in the mirror. My hair was loose around my face. I pulled it to one side and braided it like an Indian's. The face looked back at me with shadowy eyes. Talk, I said. But the face just looked at me, the way a mask does—stiff and empty.

I went out and sat down on a bench away from the others. Parents kept coming for their kids. Naomi left with her mother. The clock on the wall said 2:15. I watched Flash, who was sitting silently with a man wearing a red hunting jacket. He looked just like Flash only bigger. Right after they left Bruce came in.

"How did you get yourself into this mess?" He sat down next to me. "Do you know the police woke us all up?"

"I'm sorry."

"You're a regular Jekyll and Hyde. What were you doing in that van? I heard the police say accident and I nearly had a heart attack. I thought you'd killed yourself."

"I'm okay." My chest filled up. I knew if I looked at him, I'd end up crying.

"They told me the driver was drunk. Is that right?"

I nodded.

"Crazy kids," Bruce said.

We sat there for a moment, then he said, "What are we waiting for? Let's get out of here."

We walked out together. Me and my father. Corporal Taggert saw us leave. I was only sorry Naomi didn't see us, too.

149

Bruce drove to Connie's. The lights were on upstairs, and when we went in Connie came down in a white bathrobe.

"So you just went off in the middle of the night and ended in the police station?" Then she turned on Bruce. "What I can't understand is why he's been at the ranch all this time. Why didn't you just take him to the Y, like you said you were going to."

"What's that got to do with anything?" he said. "I knew you didn't want him under your nose, so I helped you out."

It looked like they were going to have a fight.

Then Connie said, "Okay, Bruce, let's put a lid on it. The question is, what do we do now?"

They both turned to me, as if I had the answer. I did, but they didn't want to hear it.

Connie sat down on the steps. "Why don't we just go back to the way things were?"

"You want him back here?" Bruce said. "I thought you didn't!"

"Let's just say I went temporarily nuts, as if those lies he told us meant something. He's just a kid."

"No, I'm not just a kid. I'm your son." I looked at Connie. "You're my mom. I want you to be my mom." I started crying. There was silence. I tried to dry it up. I never cried. Connie put her arms around me. Then Bruce did, too.

27

THAT WEEKEND Mary Anne threw a birthday party for Feenee, and Connie, Miller, and I drove out to the ranch. All the way there, Miller was on to Connie about a rock concert she wanted to go to. "It's going to be a mob scene," Connie said. "I don't like you going to that kind of place alone. It's not even music, Miller. It's an assault, like being beaten to death. Can't you just buy their album?"

"Mom, it's not the same thing! Francesca can only go if I go. Jason'll go, too. You want to go?" she said, turning around to me. I was sitting in the back. "Say, yes," she mouthed.

"A rock concert?" I said. "No."

I wasn't paying that much attention. I was remembering the last time I was on this road—the last two times, in fact. The first time was with Bruce when he'd driven me up to the ranch, and I thought I was on the way out. The second time was a couple of nights later, when I'd come down this same road from the ranch and thought I was never coming back.

And now everything I'd ever wanted and wished for had

suddenly been given to me. I was in the car with my mom and my sister, on the way to a birthday party for my stepsister, Feenee, Mary Anne's daughter. I loved that I even had a stepsister.

"Jason!" Miller turned. "Jason, you have to go with me. Tell Mom you're going to go."

"Sure," I said.

"You will? You just said you wouldn't."

"I changed my mind."

"Jason is going, I won't be alone. Now what do you say, Mom?"

"Can I depend on you?" Connie said to me.

I knew she was thinking back to last week and the van. "I'm not going to do anything foolish."

"There's such a mob in those places. I hate those big concerts. You'll stay with Miller?"

"To the end. You can count on me." As soon as I said it, I wanted to go as much as Miller did. Not for the concert. But to show Connie she could trust me.

"Mom?" Miller said. "Yes? Okay?"

Connie turned on Ten Turn Road. "Okay, yes. As long as you kids are going to be together."

At that moment, I never felt more like Jason.

There were balloons along the road to the ranch, tied to the mailbox, and in the trees outside the house. Connie dropped us off and said, "I'll be back for you guys in a couple of hours."

I gathered up Feenee's presents and got out of the car. I wasn't using the crutches anymore. Miller led the way around the back of the house, and we went in through the kitchen. Mary Anne was there and some people I didn't recognize. Miller went around the table and kissed each person. Then she picked up Nathan and danced around with him.

I was still holding Feenee's presents. I nudged Miller. "What do I do with these?"

"Feenee!" Miller yelled. "Presents!"

Feenee came running from the other room, grabbed the presents out of my hands and started tearing off the paper.

"Say thank you to Miller," Mary Anne said.

"Thank you," Feenee said.

"The long one is from Jason and me," Miller said. Then she went off with Nathan into the other room. I stood there wondering what I was supposed to do now. I waited for someone to ask me something, like how it felt to be home. I'd like to tell them. *Great! I have a family again. Two families! I've got a dad and two moms, two sisters, and a brother.*

"So you're Jason?" A man sitting at the table nodded at me. "I'm Uncle Walter, and this is Aunt Lila." He had a bald head and a bumpy nose. Aunt Lila had rings on all her fingers and a black curly wig that made her look like a sheep. Uncle Walter laughed. "Where have you been, Jason? That's not a very good joke, is it?"

"Who does he look like?" Aunt Lila kept saying. "There's somebody you look like."

I looked around for something to do. "You want me to do anything?" I asked Mary Anne.

"Take out the empty soda bottles and put them in the garage."

Bruce was out there. He had parked in the driveway and came in with a stack of pizzas. "Hey, Dad," I said. "Look, no crutches." I pulled up my pants leg to show him I only had on an Ace bandage.

"Good," he said and handed me the pizzas to bring in.

"Look what I found in the garage," I said to Mary Anne. She took the pizzas and slid them in the oven.

I went looking for Bruce again. He was in the living room, quieting down the kids.

Aunt Lila kept following me around. "Who does he look like? Not like you, Bruce."

Why did I have to look like anyone? "Why don't you leave me alone," I said. "I look like me. Everyone looks like themselves."

"Don't you be rude to me," Aunt Lila said.

"Get some chairs," Bruce ordered. His expression said, *And shape up!*

I stormed out to the garage. I was hot! I glared out the open doors, toward the mountains. Inside, people were talking and laughing. I was outside and everyone else was inside. The mountains gazed calmly at me. They were in the sunlight, big and quiet. Well, if you are outside, they said to me, you did it to yourself.

I took the folding chairs and went back in. Aunt Lila saw me. "He's barely civilized," she said.

"Oh, come on, now," Uncle Walter said. "He's not that bad. He's just a chip off the old block."

"You mean Bruce?" Aunt Lila said. "Never! Bruce always knew how to act with people. Him—he's like my father."

"Grandpa Diaz?" Bruce said. "I don't see that."

I set the chairs up. I felt the tension building up again. All these people looking me over and talking about me. "Acts like Grandpa, too," Aunt Lila said. "He never talked to anyone. He came home, he ate, and then he went for a walk. Company in the house, he went for a walk. All his conversation was in his feet. If you said anything to him he didn't like, he walked out."

"I'm not like that," I said.

"His hearing is good, anyway. I feel sorry for you, Bruce."

She gave me a disapproving look. "If he's like Grandpa, he'll never give you anything."

Mary Anne came around and whispered in my ear, "Give her a smile, tell her you're sorry."

"What?"

"A smile! She'll never shut up until you do."

I turned and gave Aunt Lila my best smile. "I'm sorry," I said.

She smiled back at me. "See how nice you can look when you smile. What are you going to do this summer?"

"He's going to summer school," Bruce said.

Summer school! I didn't have anything against school, but not in the summer, especially not this summer. I wanted to spend time on the ranch. I'd already told Bruce I wanted to help him here. "I'm not going to summer school," I said.

"You damn sure are. You have to make up what you missed."

Families! I walked into the other room—did just what Aunt Lila said I would do. I talked with my feet. The little kids were playing Pin the Tail on the Donkey, and screaming.

I went outside to the horses. They started showing off for me, circling the corral. It was beautiful to see them run. They were so free. But then I saw the fencing—they weren't free either. I couldn't do just anything I wanted. I had to do what Bruce said. He was the father, and he gave the orders.

Maybe that wasn't so bad. He was thinking about me. He wanted me to go to school, to get back on track. He wasn't just thinking about the summer. He was thinking about the fall and next year and maybe the rest of my life. The rest of his son's life. Jason's life. My life.

When I went back in, the little kids started yelling for Miller and me to play hide and seek with them. Feenee, the birthday girl, wanted to be "it." I hid behind a door and looked through the crack, and it was suddenly very strange. I was pressed into the narrow space behind the door, hearing the kids shrieking and smelling the pizza heating in the oven, aware that soon we'd all be sitting down together and eating. . . . And I was a part of it all.

It was like a dream.

My own family . . . sisters and a brother. Three parents. Even a weird aunt. And this house: especially the house, this warm, steamy house, where we were all together, safe, protected from the rest of the world. I crouched behind the door and thought *Here I am.* Just those three words, and they made me cry. *This is happening to somebody else. It's not me. It's somebody else's life I'm having.*

But even as I thought it, I knew it was me. I was really here. And it was like I was outside the house and inside the house at the same time. Inside looking out . . . outside looking in. I was the fish in the water and the bird in the sky. And I was afraid if I blinked it would all disappear.

PART III
WHO IS EDDIE LEONARD?

Welcome to the human race.

28

"MILLER." I RAPPED on the bathroom door. "Are you ready? Francesca and her mother are going to be here, and you'll still be in the bathroom. Are you going to this concert or not?"

"They're not coming for another ten minutes," she said through the door. "Get a grip on yourself."

"You know I hate to wait."

"It's good for your character development. Did Mom come home yet?"

"I think I just heard her car. I'll be downstairs," I said. "Hurry up! I'll meet you there."

In the hall mirror, I took a look at myself. My hair had gotten even longer and I'd tied it back with a piece of leather string. The pirate look. I liked the tail hanging down in back. It seemed to me I had gotten taller and leaner. Bony nose, bone around my eyes and above my cheeks. "You're looking good," I said to the mirror.

As I started down the stairs, I heard Connie and Bruce talking. For some reason, it made me remember Doug and

Lucy. They were nice. If I missed anyone, I missed them. I wished they could see me now. Not Eddie Leonard, but Jason Diaz. I guess I was Jason Diaz then, too, but they didn't know it. Nobody knew it, except maybe my grandmother, but I wasn't sure of that.

I heard Bruce say, "I'm sorry, Connie." There was something in his voice that made me stop and listen.

Then silence. Without knowing, I knew it was about me.

Then Bruce said, "I really am sorry. I didn't want this any more than you did."

"How do you know this is real?"

"Oh, it's real," he said. "It's genuine. It's got the state seal on it and everything."

"Why did you do it?" Connie said. "Why did you have to do it? We were happy. We had Jason back."

"No, we didn't, Connie. We never had him, no matter how much we pretended. Sooner or later we would have found out. It's his birth certificate, all right. There's his mother's name, Sharon Leonard. Not much of a mother, but she was the one. And there's the father's name. William Rush, whoever he was."

"Let's not tell him now," Connie said.

"When, then?"

"They're on their way out to a concert. When they come home, I suppose. What difference do a few more hours make?"

THE STREETS NEAR the War Memorial were clogged with cars. Francesca's mother kept inching forward, then hitting the brake. "Sorry, kids, you might be late," she said. "No way can I get through this mess. I can't go ahead. I can't go back."

Can't go ahead. Can't go back. The words repeated themselves in my head. I hated that birth certificate. I hated Eddie Leonard. I couldn't even remember him. How could I be Eddie Leonard? He was somebody I used to know. *Can't go back . . . can't go ahead.*

Francesca's mother finally maneuvered the car to a corner and let us out. "I'll meet you at the Civic Center at eleven o'clock. Francesca, are you listening?"

"I'm listening, Mother. That's what I have ears for." Francesca kicked off her high heels, took Miller's hand and started to run.

"You can't go barefoot," her mother called after her. "Jason, stop her."

I went after the girls. Miller grabbed my hand. "Come on, Jason, don't be such a poke. You're our watchdog."

As I let myself be pulled along, I remembered how proud I'd felt that Connie said she'd entrust Miller to me. The concert seemed pointless now.

The last couple of blocks the crowds were so thick, there was no running. Miller and Francesca put their heels on again. People were packed in under the marquee. A line of uniformed police stood near the ticket collectors and watched.

We inched forward. Miller held up our tickets. "Get in, get in!," Francesca kept saying. The crowd slid forward, filled the passageway and slowly emptied into the arena. It was dark inside. Long arms of light crisscrossed the ceiling. All around the stage, where the warmup band was playing, people were dancing.

We found seats toward the middle. "Can't see," Miller complained. The people in front of us were gyrating on their seats. Miller and Francesca stood up on their chairs. People were striking Bics and sending lit matches flaring out into the crowd. Miller was sweating, her hair was stuck to her skin. Her eyes shone.

The main band came on. The music shook the building. It rolled around in the dark like a giant ball, bouncing off every wall. It wrapped me up, twisted my head around, tore everything loose. *Did you really think . . . really think . . . think you were going to get away with it . . . think you were Jason . . . Jason. . . . Think again . . . think again . . .*

Miller and Francesca were screaming their heads off. All the dancing fools were in the aisles. The music stabbed at me, cut me to pieces, sliced me every which way. And in it, I heard that strange name, *Rush! William Rush*. The name on the birth certificate. *Rush . . . Rush . . . William Rush . . .* There'd been Rush kids in the school I went to. Maybe my cousins or my half brothers and sisters. A whole other story of my life.

William Rush, my father? No. When I thought father, I saw Bruce. I saw his name and Connie's blinking in the light towers above the stage. I saw Jason Diaz in electric lights. Not Eddie Leonard. Not Eddie Rush. Jason Diaz blinked above me in a dazzling light.

I couldn't hear the music anymore, but I could feel it hitting me like a steamroller. Rolling over me, then rolling back. Connie refused to call it music. She called it an assault, like being beaten to death. Connie—Mom. It was so easy to say. It rolled off my tongue like ice cream. I thought of the times we'd sat together at the piano, me beating on the bongos while she played. That was all over now. I howled with the music. I howled . . .

Miller yanked at my arm and yelled something. I was in a daze and followed her and Francesca toward the light towers and the giant black loudspeakers that rose up on either side of the stage.

29

WITH ONE HAND on Francesca's shoulder and holding Jason with the other, Miller drilled through the crowd toward the stage. The music was hip-hopping in her. She bounced. Her head bobbed and her arms and shoulders seesawed. She was hot. Her face was red and glowing. She loved the heat . . . and the closeness of the crowd . . . and the way they were all bound together by the music. Her music . . . her best friend . . . her brother. She squeezed his hand, felt bone and sinew.

The stage went dark. The crowd hushed. High above a light flickered, then opened with a little explosion of sound. White light unfolded and bent toward them. The music began—slow, joyous, high. Lights broke across the stage from left to right and right to left. The guitarists, moving fast, taking huge strides, came center stage. The thump of the bass was like the tread of a huge machine.

Miller got up on a chair. Jason braced her. Now she saw everything—the stage, the band, lights. The lead singer, in pure, perfect white, stood motionless in a wine-colored circle. He raised his arms. The guitar around his neck was like a cross, it went up, it went down, it blessed them and called them. It was a magnet drawing everything, everyone, the whole audience, toward him.

The crowd surged forward, eagerly, joyfully, rising and falling like waves that lifted Miller and carried her toward the stage. She felt she could walk on air. She lost her balance and floated down.

The wave came again. Around her, people were screaming. She was screaming. One minute it was joy, the next, terror.

The crowd, like a living creature, pressed against her. Each time it inhaled she felt herself being swallowed. Each time it exhaled, she was thrust forward.

She lost Jason. Francesca too. She wanted to stop, to find them, but she couldn't move. She was wedged in, squeezed so tight she could barely breathe. Her feet were no longer on the ground. The crowd pressed against her. She was sinking, the weight of the people around her pushing her down.

She saw a boy go down, his eyes white with terror. She saw the tendons in his neck, the delicate nostrils, perfectly shaped like the rim of a cup. People were climbing on her. She went down. Slowly down. Then, darkness.

30

AN ELBOW WAS in my throat. A boy with a pale blond mustache stared at me. We couldn't move. We were locked together like statues. I wanted to tell someone that things like this shouldn't be allowed to happen. Above us, the performers danced. People were moaning and crying. The music never stopped.

SOMEONE GRABBED MY arm and pulled me free. "You okay? Can you stand up?" I staggered away. I thought I saw Francesca's long pale hair. I yelled, but there was too much noise for her to hear me.

A cop ordered me out. "Get a medic over here," he yelled. "If you can walk, if you're not hurt, get out of here!"

"I have to find my sister."

"Clear the floor!" he yelled.

A medic in a blue uniform pushed past me. I kept trying to go back to look for Miller, but I got pushed out.

On the street, medics were bringing people out on

stretchers and loading them into the ambulances. I thought I saw Miller being carried out, and I broke through the police line and ran after the ambulance.

THE EMERGENCY WAITING ROOM was jammed. The woman at the reception desk said she didn't know anything about Miller. "Sit down. We call people by name."

I sat down, then jumped up. "Couldn't you just tell me if she's okay?"

She'd already turned to someone else.

The door to the examining rooms was blocked. Every time I went close, the guard shook his head. I waited until he looked aside and slipped in.

I walked down a long corridor, looking into each curtained cubicle. I found Miller lying on a gurney in a darkened room. "Miller." Her eyes fluttered. "It's me." I took her hand. Was she dying? I saw everything through a fog. Nothing seemed real.

A hospital aide came in. "X rays," he said. "You can wait here. We'll bring her back in a while."

I sat down, then lay down on the floor. I remembered the screams and the music and how the music became screams. Nobody knew what anybody else was doing. People were dying, and others were still dancing on the stage.

I went out into the hall. Names were being called over the PA. A doctor went by with a clipboard. Then Connie came running down the corridor. "Mom," I said. "I saw her. She's having X rays." Connie stepped around me. "Miller's having X rays," I said again. "I saw her."

Connie looked through me, then went by me as if I was invisible. "Miller," she called. "Miller."

31

I STOOD ON the street, waiting to cross. I thought about Miller and what had happened. A truck came around the corner and almost hit me. The driver stared at me like he wanted to get his hands around my throat and strangle me.

It was a long walk from the hospital to the house. I kept remembering Connie's blank look, the way she had stared through me.

The air was raw in my throat. My foot ached. I had called them family. Mom and Dad. My sister. But Bruce had been right all along. I wasn't Jason. They weren't my family. There was no family. There never had been. There was nothing but what was and what had been. . . . me and my crazy grandmother.

In the house the lights were on in every room. Graham followed me. I was hungry and drank from the juice pitcher. I felt like a burglar. *You don't belong here.* I gobbled bread down, as if someone was going to snatch it away from me.

This isn't your food, this isn't your house. I stuffed a hunk of cheese in my pocket and went back upstairs and packed my knapsack. I left a note. "Good-bye. Thanks for everything. I still love you."

32

I FOUND A JOB in a restaurant, at a place called Ernie's Diner, busing and washing dishes. I told Ernie I was eighteen. He needed a dishwasher and didn't ask a lot of questions. For a week I'd been sleeping out near the falls, but as soon as I got my first money, I rented a room in a house near the interstate. There was a gravel pit in back and trucks came and went all day and sometimes half the night.

I had thought about leaving town. It was still on my mind. There was nothing holding me here, but there was nothing drawing me anyplace either. I called the hospital, so I knew when Miller was discharged. Every day I wondered what I would do if I saw them, how I would act, what I would say.

I always imagined it would be Connie I would see first . . . and it would be the hospital all over again. Connie's eyes saying, *Who are you? You are nothing to me.*

Sometimes I thought about calling, but somehow I didn't want them to know I was here. I didn't want them to think I was asking for anything. I didn't want their pity. But there was a worse thought—that they didn't pity me, that they didn't even think about me anymore.

My room in Mrs. Pritkin's house was upstairs in back with a view of the gravel pit. I had a bed, a chair, and an oak bureau with a faded mirror. The wallpaper was peeling and watermarked where rain had leaked through the roof. I kept the windows closed most of the time to muffle the sound of the trucks.

There was one other roomer, a truck driver, John Cooper. He lived downstairs. I didn't see him a lot. Sometimes I'd hear him come in from the road. I'd hear the hiss of brakes, and then I'd look out the window and see the trailer lights on the truck. I was always glad when he was back. It didn't seem so lonely in the house.

I asked John one time how he got his job. Where had he learned to drive big trucks? "On the job, Jason," he said. I'd given Mrs. Pritkin and John my name as Jason Leonard. "I was a helper," John said. In back of my mind was the thought that maybe I could be his helper. I didn't want to always work in Ernie's. All the people who worked there were old. Ernie did all the cooking, and he was in back most of the time. "Hey, kid," he'd yell, when he wanted me to do something. Or else he'd say, "Where's that boy?" Sometimes I cut vegetables if Marie, the salad lady, had to baby-sit her granddaughter. Dishes and tables and keeping the floor clear were my main duties. Everybody was always giving me orders. "Get this . . . get that . . ." Once or twice I felt like quitting, but then it was like I heard Bruce in my head. *So you get ordered around—so what? Do the job.*

I stayed on, but it was still pretty dull. If I ever got to be John's helper, I could travel, make money, see the country. And there would always be this place to come home to. I saw myself swinging the big trailer around the house, then nosing it out toward the road before I cut the power and the lights. I daydreamed about that a lot.

Sometimes I thought about the house on Walcott Street. Some day, I thought, I'd just walk by, but not on their side of the street. But then I thought that Graham would sniff me out anyway, and Miller would come out and see me. And then—? I didn't know. I thought Miller would understand, and maybe we'd pick right up where we'd left off.

It was hard to stay away. I had to stop myself from picking up the phone. Once I dialed, then broke the connection, afraid that I'd break down and beg them to take me back.

On my time off, I went to a lot of movies. I bought clothes. I spent time in the library, reading the newspapers and magazines. Sometimes I took a book out. The best thing, though, was when I met a girl. No, I didn't meet her. I saw her in George Thornton Park. She was with a bunch of kids on skateboards.

She wore a big sweater and knee protectors, and her hair went down her back. She didn't do anything dazzling on the board, but she was okay. The guys were jumping over garbage cans and riding up on the curb. But she sailed around, arms out, with a calm, peaceful face. I went back to the park. I saw her a few times, but then she stopped coming.

Working for Phil Horton was the next job I got. He was tall and he wore belted white overalls and a painter's cap. I met him on the street one day. He had an old dented Chevy panel truck stuffed with ladders and drop cloths and paints. I stopped to talk to him. He had stuff out on the street that he had to get inside to an apartment in a hurry, and I helped him carry it in.

"Thanks, kid. What's your name?"

"My name?" I said. "My name's Leonard."

"You looking for a job, Leonard?"

"I might be. What do you have in mind?"

"I need a helper, someone I can depend on. Do you like to paint?"

"Sure," I said. What was there to painting a wall? So I started working four days a week for Ernie and weekends with Phil. He had two jobs, himself, and he couldn't keep up with everything. He said once I learned the ropes I could be painting on one job and he could be checking on another or doing an estimate, lining up new work.

We got along great. Sometimes we worked through the whole day and didn't even stop to eat. Afterward, he'd take me to a grill on Hudson Avenue, where he went all the time, and treat me to supper. "You like chili, Leonard?" he said.

"I don't care one way or the other. To me, it's all hash and potatoes."

We sat at the counter and he ordered for both of us. We were in our work clothes. His glasses were spattered with white paint. "I don't see how you can see at all," I said.

"I can see that your face is freckled white. We both look like a couple of clowns."

He ordered beer for us. "You get dry working," he always said. "Painters drink a lot."

One day Phil sent me back to his house for extra drop cloths. He told me to take the truck—I'd been driving it a little, and I had my permit. In the truck, my mind started working. I had wheels. I could go anywhere. I imagined driving up to the house on Walcott Street and honking the horn. Or going by Miller's school and parking outside. But I just drove to Phil's house and then back to the job.

33

SOMETIMES MILLER WOULD close her eyes and things came to her that she didn't want to think about. The concert . . . the way the crowd had pressed forward . . . the weight of people on every side . . . being unable to turn or break free or move . . . For a long time after the concert, she slept a lot. In health class Mrs. Leader said that the growth hormones worked best while you slept. Miller wouldn't mind growing, but mostly she was tired. Her mother got worried and took her to the doctor again. The doctor said that after a trauma like the one Miller had endured, her body needed time to recover.

Sometimes she thought about Jason, and she'd feel so sad she'd put the pillow over her face. She wanted to talk about him, but nobody else did. When she thought of Jason, she saw Eddie. When she thought of Eddie, she saw Jason. She couldn't separate them. Before, she'd had nothing but a picture of a three year old. Now, she had Eddie to fill in all the empty places. They showed her Eddie's birth certificate.

"He was lying to us all along," her father said. Miller tried to talk to her mother about where Jason—or Eddie—could have gone. "I don't know," her mother said. "I don't want to think about him." And that was it.

Some nights Miller couldn't sleep. Her ribs bothered her, and she sat up and read until her eyes blurred. Other nights, she was so tired that when she closed her eyes she fell instantly asleep. But then she'd have bad dreams. She'd wake up, sit up in bed. It was quiet in the room. The dream was still in her head—the screams, the sirens. She held her side as she went to the window. Outside, the garage stood as it always did, half hidden by trees.

Where was he sleeping tonight? Once, he'd told her he could sleep anywhere. He said he could lie down in the snow or crawl under a rock and sleep like a wolf. Boasting. He was always showing off, making himself out big and macho. Once they'd talked about traveling together, and he'd said they could go from one end of the country to the other, and they'd never have to spend a penny. They'd find shelter in barns and live on wild apples and food people threw out in restaurants. "When we come to the borders of states," he had said, "we'll stand with one foot in one state and one foot in the other."

She pulled on her sneakers and went downstairs, suddenly convinced that he was here. She went out to the garage. Graham went with her, as if he knew, too. She opened the door to the garage, and he ran up the stairs to the loft. Then he appeared above her, looking puzzled. "Nobody there?" she said. She went up to look for herself, then sat on the stairs with Graham.

34

IN SEPTEMBER, PHIL and I worked on a house only five blocks from Walcott Street. Almost five months since I'd left and I hadn't seen them once. There were mums in bloom in front of the house we were painting, and the days we worked, it rained a lot. I could have walked over to Walcott Street anytime, but what would be the use of it?

It's hard to wake up and face what's true. It's hard to open your eyes and know that you're still in the same place you've always been. It's hard to give up dreams. It's hard not to want a real family. It's hard to give it up when you think you've found it. It's hard to walk away and say it's all right when it isn't.

Sometimes I thought I couldn't have done anything else but what I did. And sometimes I couldn't understand how I ever got myself into the whole thing. I'd really believed it. Believed I was Jason Diaz. I *was* Jason Diaz while I lived there. And they believed it, too. It was wonderful and I'd been happy and loved them. Connie and Miller and Bruce. They were my family. When I was with them, everything in my life seemed to make sense. Miller had called me brother. Connie had been my mother.

If only it had been true. It could have been true. It was only a piece of paper that made it untrue. Eddie Leonard's birth certificate. I wasn't Jason, but I didn't feel like Eddie Leonard anymore. Then who was I? Phil called me Leonard. At my job in the restaurant, I was "the boy." And where I lived, Mrs. Pritkin and John called me Jay or Jason.

One night Phil and I were in the Hudson Avenue grill, and we'd had a bottle of beer before the food came, when the girl I'd seen skating in George Thornton Park came in. She was with a couple of guys and the waitress seemed to know them. They sat down by the window. Phil and I were at the counter. The girl had on a heavy cardigan and her hair pulled back. She looked Spanish, a lot of dark around her eyes. Large eyes. Amazing eyes. She caught me looking at her, and she looked away, but not too fast.

Before I lost my nerve, I went over to her. I was scared, but what did that matter? "I saw you skating once in George Thornton Park." I nodded at the two guys. "I like the way you skate. Do you go over to that park a lot?"

"Are you a skateboarder?"

"Me? No, but I like to watch. Maybe I'll see you around again," I said, and I went back to the counter.

I didn't look her way again, afraid I would spoil what I'd started. Maybe I was dreaming, but I knew I was going to see her again, and she'd remember me the next time. Phil offered me a ride home, but I wanted to be alone. The clock high on the White Insurance Building said ten o'clock. I went down the nearly empty streets, past shuttered and barred stores, under the scaffolding of a new building. A huddled figure in a doorway startled me. Someone was sleeping there. Someone alone and without a family. It could have been me.

I thought of the girl. Why hadn't I asked her name? I should have told her mine. Eddie Leonard. No, I didn't like that name. "I'm a painter," I could have said. "Just call me splash, splatter, and drip." She would have laughed. I felt high, I bounced along, my knapsack knocking against my back. I felt I could do anything, as if I'd doubled in size, stepped out of a little box into a box so big I could hardly fill it.

Had I said enough to her? Too much? Oh, it sure wasn't too much! I should have told her some interesting things. I could have told her how I'd been searching for my true family and I was still searching. She would have been interested.

I borrowed Phil's truck now and then at lunch. After I picked up our sodas and sandwiches, I'd drive by the park and just check it out. Then I'd cross town and go by Miller's school. One day, there were a lot of kids outside and a couple of big yellow school buses parked in front. A teacher, the same one who'd kept me out of the building, was using his hands as a megaphone. "Everyone going to the movie, get on the bus *now*."

I saw Miller getting on the bus with Francesca. I could have called out to her. I thought of getting out of the truck and going over to the bus. I didn't know what I'd say to her. Maybe I'd just wave hello. Would she be glad to see me, or would she turn away? I didn't realize until then how afraid I was of that. And I didn't realize, until I saw the bus pull away, how much I missed her. Of everyone, I missed her the most. I missed her being my sister. I missed being her brother.

35

AFTER WORK ONE DAY Phil asked me to go shopping with him. He was on the outs with his girlfriend, and he wanted me to help him buy her something that would soften her up. "She likes presents and she likes surprises," he said. "I need some advice." But when we got to the mall, he found what he wanted right away without my advice. It was a miniature ceramic owl.

"What's the use of it?" I said. "What's she going to do with it?"

"She's a nut about owls. Her house is full of them."

I needed jeans and some other stuff, but I didn't want to go in any of the stores in my painting clothes. "Leonard, don't worry, they'll still take your money," Phil said. He more or less dragged me into Chambers Department Store, where I got the things I needed.

We were on our way out when I saw Miller. We walked right into each other. "Jason?" she said. For a minute, I couldn't think straight.

"Jason?" Phil said.

"Phil," I said, "this is Miller." I didn't know what he thought, but I didn't really care. "Listen, I'll call you tonight."

"You don't want a ride home?"

"No, I'm okay." I was looking at Miller.

"Who's he?" Miller said, after Phil left.

"My boss. He's my friend, too. He's a nice guy."

"Your boss? You're working?"

"You don't think I look like this all the time? How have you been?" I said. "I've been thinking about you."

"I thought you forgot all about us."

"That's funny, I thought you forgot about me."

"Why would I do that?" she said. She kept looking at me. "Jason," she said, "I can't believe you're here!" Suddenly she screamed and thrust her face into mine, hugged me and kissed me.

It was great after that. We walked around, and we talked and talked. We stopped for ice cream cones and sat down at one of the tables and talked some more. "Did you know?" she said. "I mean, all the time that you were with us, did you know that you weren't really Jason?"

"No."

She looked at me for a moment. "Really?"

"Really."

She licked off the ice cream drips. "I believe you," she said.

My eyes started to smart. "You do?"

"Yes," she said. "Of course I do."

A FEW NIGHTS LATER, I'd just come out of the shower when Mrs. Pritkin called up to me that I had a phone call. I pulled on jeans and a shirt and ran downstairs. The phone was in the hall. I thought it was Phil about our job tomorrow.

"Eddie, this is Connie."

"Connie," I said.

"Miller told me she met you. How are you?"

"Fine." Suddenly I wanted a cigarette. I hadn't smoked since that day I threw away my pack at Connie's house.

"Miller says you're working. I'm disappointed you're not in school."

I didn't know what to say to that. "I have to pay rent and buy food," I said. "I'm doing okay." Hearing her voice, I was on the verge of breaking down. I kept going to the edge, then pulling back.

"Will you come see us?" she said.

"I don't know." I felt as if something was stuck in my throat. My feelings kept coming up on me. She'd taken me in, then kicked me out. I'd been her son, then I'd been nothing.

"I never thought that you'd just disappear that way. Why did you do that?"

"I left you a note," I said.

"Yes, that was nice, but you might as well have disappeared off the face of the earth." She was silent for a moment. "Don't you know you're special to me?"

Special? If I was so special, why didn't she tell me to come home?

"Eddie?" she said. "Are you still there?"

I looked down the hall to the living room, where Mrs. Pritkin was watching TV. "I'm here."

"This is hard," she said. Then abruptly, "I need to come clean with you. How can I say it to you without hurting you more? I'm just going to say it. I know you want to come back. I'm right, aren't I?"

"No, I'm okay." What did she want? Did she want me to

say it was okay that I couldn't live with them? That I understood? Okay, I understood. But it didn't make it any easier to accept. I'd loved living in her house. I'd loved being her son. I'd never forget that.

"What I'm trying to say is that you're still important to me. If you ever need anything . . . It isn't as if you're a stranger—"

"Thanks," I said. "I've got to hang up."

"No, wait, Eddie! I didn't say that right. I care about you. I care about you a lot. I want us to be friends. Can you believe that?"

I didn't answer.

"Eddie?"

I hung up.

I WENT DOWN TO the phone later and called Phil, woke him up. I heard him say something to somebody and then he said "What? What happened?" And I told him the whole story, beginning to end. I didn't even turn on the light. I just stood there in the dark and talked.

"So this is what it's all about," he said. "They lost their kid and they've been looking for him all these years. Then you come along, a boy looking for a family. Bingo! You both got what you want. What a story! I knew there was something going on with you. And that girl you met in the mall—she's in that family?"

"Yes, that's Miller."

"Now I'm going to tell you something. As long as they thought there was a chance you might be their son, they could accept you. They could handle that. But once they knew, once they got their hands on that birth certificate, they didn't want you."

"Right," I said. He wasn't telling me anything I didn't know. I was waiting for something else, some words of wisdom.

"The whole world is like that," Phil said. Maybe he thought he was cheering me up. "Welcome to the human race. You're either an insider or an outsider. You either belong or you don't belong. You didn't belong to those people. You weren't their flesh and blood. Even though you were flesh and blood just like them. So what are you going to do now?"

"Just what I'm doing."

"Just remember, if you don't have a family, you can always have friends. You got friends, good friends like me. No, I mean it, and don't you forget it. Friends mean a lot in this world. Hang on to your friends."

"Right," I said.

"Count 'em," Phil ordered. "How many have you got?"

"You," I said.

"That's all?"

"Maybe Barbara." She was Phil's girlfriend.

"So you got two friends," Phil said. "Better than none."

"Right." Then I thought of John, the truck driver, and Mrs. Pritkin, my landlady. And how about Ernie and all the old pests working with him—they were a good lot. I shouldn't forget Lucy and Doug, either. One of these days I'd go back to see them. And Miller—definitely, Miller. She was always going to be my friend. Connie and Bruce? I didn't know about them. That was hard. Maybe, someday.

"You still there?" Phil said. "I want to tell you one more thing. I'm your best friend, but you call me up this late again and I'm going to break your neck."

36

I SAW THE SKATEBOARD girl one day waiting at a bus stop downtown. I was on my way to meet Phil and his girlfriend, Barbara. We were all going to a movie together. "Where's your skateboard?" I called.

She looked puzzled for a second, then she recognized me. "Oh! Hi."

"Where're you going?"

"None of your business."

"Listen, I feel like I know you," I said. "I'm going to a movie. Want to come with me?"

"No! Are you crazy? My brothers would kill me if I did that."

"Those two guys were your brothers? Oh, that's good. I thought so, but I wasn't sure. They aren't going to kill you. They know me, too."

That made her laugh. "Well, good-bye," she said.

"Wait a minute, wait a minute. What's your name? I want to see you again."

"You're such a funny guy," she said. "Marie Bagorian."

"Marie Bagorian," I repeated. "I'll never forget it."

"Tell me your name."

"My name?" For a moment I wanted to say Jason Diaz. I wanted her to like me. She would like Jason Diaz, whose father was a dentist and who had a cute kid sister and lived in a house on Walcott Street. Eddie Leonard—what did he have? A rented room, high school dropout, no parents, no sibs, only a crazy grandmother who was dead.

"What do you have to know my name for?" I said. "What's in a name?"

"You're not going to tell me your name after I told you mine? What's the matter, did you do something bad?"

"What if I said my name was Jason Diaz?"

"That's a nice name."

"Just testing. How about Eddie Leonard?"

"Which one? Jason or Eddie?"

"You choose," I said.

"Oh, no. That's ridiculous . . . Oh, there's my bus." She signaled it, and it slowed down. "Well, good-bye," she said.

"I'm Eddie," I said. "I'm someone named Eddie."

"Are you sure? You're cute, Eddie."

"Eddie Leonard."

"Not Jason?" The bus stopped, and the door opened. "You sure?"

"I'm sure. I'll tell you the whole story someday, if we get to be friends."

"Okay, Eddie Leonard," she said. She got on the bus. " 'Bye, Eddie Leonard."

It sounded good when she said it.

About the Author

HARRY MAZER is the author of many acclaimed novels for young adults, including *Snow Bound, The Last Mission, The Dollar Man, The Island Keeper* and *Someone's Mother Is Missing,* all published by Delacorte Press and available in Dell Laurel-Leaf editions. Mr. Mazer and his wife, novelist Norma Fox Mazer, are the authors of *The Solid Gold Kid, Heartbeat,* and *Bright Days, Stupid Nights,* published in Bantam Starfire editions.

The Mazers have four grown children and divide their time between Syracuse, New York, and New York City.